Doom, Gloom and Despair

Tales to horrify and amuse

Aaron Aalborg

Penman House Publishing

Published by Penman House Publishing

ISBN: 978-0-9908764-4-1

Typesetting services by BOOKOW.COM

To the late Greg Bascom author of 'Lawless Elements', a Faulkner Prize-winning novel. He taught me a lot and will be missed by many.

ACKNOWLEDGMENTS

My thanks are due to my friends and fellow authors at Penman House Publishing, K. Francis Ryan and Michael Crump, for helping at every stage of the conception and completion of these stories in ways too numerous to mention.

As always, my wife Ivy deserves my undying gratitude for tolerating my aberrant behavior during writing, or maybe all the time, and for support with editing. There were many people who read one or more of the stories and gave useful feedback. I thank them all. Thanks also to my editor Jenny Kitson. She kept me from the chaos which is my lack of version control.

INTRODUCTION

"Happiness was but the occasional episode in a general drama of pain"

Thomas Hardy - 'The Mayor of Casterbridge'

Each of the short stories in this compilation is intended to amuse or horrify and sometimes both. They are as dark as you can get. You have been warned.

Keep this volume out of the hands of children, dogs and bears. It might give them ideas.

Those with depressive natures and suicidal tendencies should definitely read and study this book. It will fully justify your melancholia. If you do decide to end it all, you will be completely satisfied that you are correct in your choice. You may even feel a little superior to others who choose to continue humanity's pointless plague on this planet.

If you have any doubts, recite this cheery mantra several times a day.

**"Hurrah! Hurrah! Hurrah!
Things will get worse by far"**

There is a reason why this book is a series of short stories rather than in my usual novel form. It is because, if you kill off all the characters, you are forced to keep starting again.

DISCLAIMER

Aaron Aalborg is not responsible for any actions taken after reading this book. Indeed, he is totally irresponsible. All lawsuits so far have been successfully defended with insanity pleas.

Save the Planet 1

The End of Hypocrisy

"Hypocrite reader, my fellow, my brother"

Charles Baudelaire

Lenny looked appraisingly at the fellow members of the local green action group. Then he ran his eyes along the row of enormous SUVs and high-end cars the members had parked on his capacious parking circle in Greenwich, Connecticut.

Were they ready for his new idea? Perhaps not, maybe they were too comfortable in their planet-despoiling lifestyles to accept that they were the problem; not Monsanto, not Exxon, not even the government. But he had to try.

Giving a loud cough, he interrupted the social chitchat. Ruth quickly stuffed a huge piece of lemon drizzle cake in her mouth, as Lenny was always rather long-winded. Once he started, she would be unable to take more without being noticed. The others swiveled their heads towards him.

He possessed that charisma; that way with words; that power of ideas, which commanded their universal respect and attention. Today, the fire in his eyes was especially compelling.

"Let's review what we've achieved in the last three years. What have we actually done to stop global warming?"

Ruth piped up smugly, wiping crumbs from her mouth, "Well, some of us have bought electric cars."

The others looked enviously at her shiny new Tesla SUV parked outside, near the artificial waterfall and fountain. The vehicle combined a statement of her wealth with the merest curtsy to her self-sacrifice to save the planet.

Lenny pricked her bubble. "You're right Ruth. Several of us have hybrids or electric cars, among the four or five others in each of our garages. Is that really helping the planet? Think of the metals, plastics and other scarce resources consumed to make them."

Ruth caught the smirks that one or two of the others tried to hide and shot back. "True, but at least we use less fossil fuel and the Tesla has many recyclable components."

Lenny smiled and raised his hands in conciliation. "It's a start of course, but this past year was another record hot one. Our choice of transport did not quite do the trick."

Walter gave him an appreciative look. Lenny's position as the leader of a gay rights group, his Bostonian drawl and Harvard PhD had merited the group's admiration. He also had one of the most elegant and extensive mansions in Greenwich where he entertained this group as well as many from the political and movie elite. "Well, we stopped them building the waste incineration plant in Cos Cob. That prevented any chance of PCBs polluting our surroundings. It also removed the risks of heavy metals from the residual ash leaching into the ground water."

Lenny acknowledged this with a friendly nod. "Thanks Walt. That's a great example of how we look after our immediate backyard. But our trash still has to go somewhere. In this case, the contractor is now shipping it by sea. Who knows what happens to it then. It could end up in the ocean or Africa for all we know. We've all heard of similar cases.

"I've been thinking a lot lately. Here's something to read before I share my idea. Then we can discuss it."

He passed around some papers that he had copied. Each member of the group studied them in silence for a few moments. One or two frowned. Ruth shrugged.

Our Contributions to Global Warming

1) Dwellings greater than the average size for North America.

- Use of construction and maintenance materials

- Fuel for air-conditioning, house heating and swimming pools

- Destruction of habitat

2) Vehicles - several per family, which consume materials and fuel.

3) Use of air transport for business and vacations. Our carbon footprints are horrific.

4) Food

- Production and waste

- Packaging

- Transportation and storage

5) …

The list went on for several pages. The group looked sheepishly at each other. Lenny raised his voice a notch. "We are the problem, each and every one of us. Does any one disagree?"

Irrepressible, Ruth jumped in. "That's all very well but what do you suggest we do? We can't all live in caves and grow our own food."

Lenny's eyes flashed with enthusiasm and he spoke excitedly, upping the pace. "Well we can continue to live as we do and accept that we are really just a discussion group, which collectively spends enough on monthly dog grooming to feed an Indian village for a year. Or we can decide we really mean it and change the future of the planet."

"The others looked doubtful, but as usual, Lenny's powerful presence won him a hearing. To increasing levels of agitation and some incredulity, Lenny spent the next hour sharing his big idea. His incontrovertible arguments and powerful personality led even the more skeptical members to start to nod in agreement towards the end.

* * *

It was mid-October. Lenny was slated to speak at a pumpkin festival in Beacon, up the Hudson River from New York City. He had thought to combine his appearance at the festival with a little leaf peeping, as the fall leaves were in their full glory of crimsons, golds and yellows.

His support team had miscalculated. A cold snap had brought early snow flurries and despite the sunshine, many people had stayed away. The wide Hudson reflected the dull grey clouds. Those braving the chill were bundled up.

Still, friends texting friends about Lenny's appearance had resulted in a decent crowd. A smiling Lenny toured the stalls followed by a doting entourage. He drank hot cinnamon cider from one stall, which benefited from an immediate boost in sales. He dutifully trudged round others selling mud colored clothing made from natural fibers, ear-flapped hats from the Andes and beads woven into peace symbols.

He lingered at a stall plugging wind power, attracted by a petite blonde with a red nose from the chill. She was surprised by the jostling crowd around her stall, but showed Lenny the two key pages in her sales folder. "This is one of our windmills. We have several in the area. The other photograph shows where your power comes from now."

The second picture was a montage of several power generation stations. Their tangled pipework, belching smokestacks, and filth contrasted with the shiny lone windmill. Lenny asked, "Is the station in the corner of the page Indian Point?"

"Yes it's a first generation nuclear station with an appalling accident record that is still being used decades past its design life. It provides power to New York City only a few miles downstream. Indian Point is a catastrophe waiting to happen."

He smiled at the girl. "Excellent! Come on everyone. Sign up for this. Help to save the planet."

She was busy with her forms till they ran out. Lenny moved towards the small stage where an aged hippy woman was droning out a dismal folk song as a tribute to Pete Seeger. He had once lived in Beacon. Her audience comprised five dutiful family members, who rapidly moved aside to allow Lenny's swarming disciples to take the rows of white plastic seats.

Lenny lit up the crowd with his ideas and enthusiasm for saving the planet to tumultuous acclaim. A local TV crew captured some key sound bites and an interview for their evening news show. Texts from the audience reached thousands of others.

* * *

A year later, the small township of Van Linton in the Connecticut countryside had been transformed. At the town boundaries, Green signage boldly announced, "We will save the Planet."

A shiny new processing plant stood at the edge of the town. Accommodation for the many short-term visitors had sprung up around the old white clapboard church, which was now a large meeting room.

Lenny was addressing the two hundred people in the fourth intake. A few of his original green group were still around and acted as ushers. They dutifully initiated the clapping as he emphasized his points with messianic eyes and emphatic gestures. Some compared his bearded face to that of Jesus or maybe Moses.

His audience had seen his videos on the Internet. Many present had contributed their life savings to the movement. All were electrified to be face to face with their prophet and the likely savior of the planet. They cheered him to the wooden trusses supporting the roof.

* * *

Next morning the processing began. In a large clinically white room, separated by stainless steel doors from the production line, each volunteer signed a consent form. Two of the movement's doctors countersigned them. Smiling nurses in white uniforms with the green Save the Planet logo on their caps, handed out the pills.

The intake started to feel drowsy and happy as they were helped through the doors at the end of the room.

* * *

Ten years later, in Yankee Stadium, Lenny was addressing the annual world convention of the movement. Loudspeakers and enormous repeater screens ensured that all could see and hear. The telecast was being transmitted worldwide. He smiled into the cameras. "This past year has been the most successful to date. Our production finally reached our target of 1 billion last year and this year we expect to comfortably beat that.

"We offer great respect and thanks to the Young Dalai Lama. Pope Joan II and to Grand Ayatollah Mhanahi, who all volunteered last year."

Each of the three saintly clerics appeared in turn on the screens, with a green and gold halo behind their heads. Cheering crowds of saffron-garbed monks in Lhasa greeted the Dalai Lama's image. The distinctive, forward-curving headgear of the two rival Tibetan traditions was picked out by the cameras. One group's hats were red and the other yellow. The monks seemed to be competing in their wild cheering. The deep base notes of their huge Dungchen trumpets briefly silenced those in the stadium.

Pope Joan's elfin beauty garnered ecstatic applause. The thousands crammed into St. Peter's Square, Rome flourished flags bearing the logo of the movement, superimposed with a green Christian Cross.

In Tehran, smiling Ayatollahs waved to Shiite devotees. Black clad and bearded Republican Guards fired their Kalashnikovs into the air in exuberant celebration.

Lenny held up his hands for silence. "Because we have long had laws in the US permitting extraordinary rendition and imprisonment without trial, we have been able to increase production to include the last of the fugitive senators, the remaining members of Congress and the employees of the NSA, CIA and FBI. Our armed forces are closing in on the final resistance groups in the Rockies."

The stadium erupted in cheering and waving of rattles. The well-known and despised leaders of Congress and the Senate stared dejectedly at the cameras. They stood in lines with sagging shoulders and miserable faces at the entrance to a processing plant somewhere in America.

* * *

That evening, Lenny made love to a group of his prettier and younger acolytes. As usual his ambition exceeded his stamina and some were disappointed. He found that these 'after parties' helped release the tension from the stress of his performance. He was not as young as he once was and rousing his followers left him drained.

They had had to stop the anything-goes mass orgies for the volunteers. The degree to which their inhibitions fell away on volunteering had been remarkable. However, some had changed their minds about enrolling and caused disruptions after hooking up in these events.

Later, Lenny would pass the files of those girls who lacked sufficient devotion and enthusiasm to his loyal Chief Operating Officer. He was blithely unaware of the jealous looks he often received from that man. He was the number two in the movement. Lenny trusted him completely.

Lenny smiled to himself. There seemed to be an endless supply of eager female acolytes happy to please him before moving on to save the planet. He was just falling into a fitful slumber with a bronzed and toned thigh draped over his leg when the door to his room burst open. A hood was roughly pushed over his head. He was frog-marched out, gripped by powerful hands. His muffled protests were ignored.

* * *

As the hood was whipped off, he screamed. The doors of the processing plant opened. His ankles were chained. He was the first in a line of a thousand others. A hook whizzed up from a slot in the floor to engage his chain. Suddenly, he was upside down with the blood rushing to his head. An overhead conveyor carried the volunteers inexorably along towards the whirling, slaughtering knives.

The others in this batch were doped and placid. The Beatles were singing 'All you need is love' over the loud speakers. Lenny desperately hurled himself backwards and forwards from his hook, bellowing his anger and roaring for help. The chain cut into his ankles with each frantic swing.

No one could hear him. He remembered that he had decided that the job of slaughtering was too dehumanizing. The plants were completely automated. He let out a long last scream as a horizontal band knife deftly slit his throat. Other blades eviscerated him before he lost consciousness.

* * *

An hour and a half later, yet another container of meat products joined the many being assembled at the New York container port. Some of these forty-foot metal boxes were marked 'Halal'. One was even stenciled 'Kosher'.

The ship with the green logo on its funnel was to sail from the New York Terminal, en route to the starving in Africa and India. The meat was free range of course. Lenny had finally made his contribution to saving the planet.

* * *

A month later asteroid X238 hit the Sahara desert with the force of a trillion Hiroshima bombs. The Earth was smashed into a myriad of incandescent rocks, hurtling towards the edge of the galaxy.

The End

Homage to Coming Up for Air

"And it's a wonderful thing to be a boy, to go roaming where grown-ups can't catch you, and to chase rats and kill birds and shy stones and cheek carters and shout dirty words"

George Orwell, *Coming Up for Air*

Under a leaden sky, Albert sat with his head in his hands, on a bench by the side of Syke Pond in Rochdale, Lancashire. An empty, quarter-bottle of cheap whisky lay on the grass by his side. It had not helped. It had dulled his senses, but he was as depressed as ever.

He watched a happy kid on the other side of the pond who was playing with a toy sailing boat.

Albert mused about himself taking the same simple pleasure forty years previously. His smaller yacht had been blue-painted wood with white sails. This lad had a modern plastic version with a remote control for steering. Albert's yacht had simply sailed wherever the wind blew. That entailed lots of running round the pond to catch the boat with a hook as it was about to hit the other side, grazing its hull on the stone edge of the pond.

Albert remembered the time when a gust of wind blew his dad's light grey trilby hat into the pond. They had to wait for it to float to the other side, blown like a slow barge. Dad had clipped him round the ear for laughing. Much had happened since then.

* * *

In retrospect, Albert traced the start of his troubles to a row in New York with his wife of 15 years. He had consumed a six-pack of Bud while watching a Mets game on TV and was starting on another. Her raucous voice was constantly interrupting him. "Can't you turn that down?

"Sandra's comin' round tonight. I'll need the sitting room. You'll have to go to your den.

"How d'ya like these new pants?"

Irritated by this last question and emboldened with drink, he gave the foolish response that set him on the path to his doom. "Well it doesn't do much for yer fat ass."

Bronx women are not known for their gentle reticence. She had stormed out. The plate of pizza she had thrown at him left a dent and tomato stains on the wall. The matching stains on his Mets T-shirt would never wash out. He had continued to watch the game, enjoying the relative peace and foolishly hoping that would be the end of the matter.

Following Albert's insult, his wife was determined to tone up and lose weight. She started making daily trips to the gym and watching her diet. Four weeks later, she moved in with her personal trainer. The divorce cost him the house and a lot more.

* * *

He remembered how things had gone down hill from then on. In the winters of the four years prior to the fatal Mets game, he and his beer-bellied mates had taken a 'fishing' trip to the warmer climes of Central America. Each vacation followed the same pattern.

The buddies began by checking into rooms in a well-known sports bar hotel. As they sipped their first martinis, pretty young hookers would sidle up to get acquainted. Invariably, three days later, out of Viagra, utterly drained of energy and with most of their cash gone, the friends would visit the coast to ensure that they had some fishing photographs. Then they flew home exhausted, with silly smiles on their faces.

Visiting the doc to check for STDs was always a little worrying, but only one of them ever had a problem. He became the butt of ribald jokes for weeks afterwards. A course of antibiotics had ended his misery.

One year, they hired a gringo wildlife expert for a change. They hiked puffing along forest trails and spent the evenings drinking with him in his favorite beach bar. Both he and his young lady friends were really hospitable. All this had left Albert with happy memories of life in Central America.

* * *

Post divorce, he could no longer afford to live in Manhattan. He decided to move to the Central America he remembered so fondly from those previous forays. Everyone there was so friendly and eager to help. The Latinas were pretty and willing. He thought that he could continue his computer work via the Internet. Perfect.

Being a cautious fellow, he decided to read some of the many books on moving to his new location.

He watched enticing YouTube videos showing endless sun, pristine beaches and pretty girls. The books and movies raved about the climate, the low costs, the simplicity of life and the ease of transition. Some featured portly Americans in Hawaiian shirts turning sizzling steaks on their barbecues.

These red-faced gringos were always surrounded by happy smiling friends, clutching exotic cocktails and generally having a great time among tropical flowers and lush vegetation. Usually there was a swimming pool, complete with shapely local girls.

To make doubly sure he was doing the right thing, he took a relocation tour with other enthusiastic gringos, keen to escape the daily grind of their various US cities. Some hated the freezing winters of their northern homes. Others could not afford the spiraling costs of healthcare and property taxes in the US.

They were led to believe that social medicine in this paradise was high quality and cheap. A number just hated the broken US political system and believed that Central America offered a haven of peace and happiness. If they were Republicans, they were seeking freedom from the grasping hands of government. If they were Democrats they wanted to escape the perceived bigotry and harshness of the US system, with its focus on wealth and consumption.

During the tour, they were introduced to realtors and compatriots who had already made the move. Each night they had a rare old time swopping yarns over innumerable rum cocktails. In their cups, one or two of the group confided that they wanted to dodge paternity suits, alimony or IRS problems. Several were looking for third or fourth wives from among the Latinas. They understood that each of these girls was keen to snag a gringo with money even if he was old enough to be her father, but making the selection was going to be fun.

* * *

Albert returned to New York convinced and eager. He was especially taken with a smiling blonde realtor. She had given him her card with a wink saying in a husky voice, "You really must come back. I could show you around."

He could not get her out of his mind and frequently looked at her photograph on the card. Her café au lait suntan, the tilt of her long neck, showing through blond hair and her plunging necklines excited his dreams. He called her. His heart quickened at that sexy Texas drawl. "Come on down. We'll have a great time and I'll show you some properties."

* * *

Four weeks later, he was wrapping up his affairs in New York. Things had gone incredibly smoothly.

He was expecting to move into the second house she had showed him. It was the one with the fantastic mountain and sea views, a sunny terrace and an infinity pool. He telephoned her to finalize arrangements and got his first shock.

"I've bad news for you Al, the lawyer acting for the buyer isn't returning my calls. The vendor says he hasn't received your deposit and wants to pull out of the deal."

Albert broke into a sweat stammering, "Jesus, all my liquid assets went into that deposit. What the hell am I supposed to do now?"

"You'd better come down here right away, so we can sort it all out."

* * *

Six months later, he still had not recovered his deposit. The lawyer had resurfaced claiming Albert had reneged on the deal.

Other lawyers played him along. "Sure, I can help you. My fee will be a thousand dollars."

Then, after several thousand dollars more and no progress, he took a call from the lawyer who had his deposit. "Listen señor. You are wasting your time annoying me. The judges are my friends. Courts take years to deal with matters here. You've been saying bad things about me. You can either drop the matter or I'll have you arrested for criminal libel. You should consider your personal safety here too."

Albert spoke with a sun-wizened gringo in the hotel bar. The guy was a long time resident and wise to local ways. He advised Albert to drop the case. "The law only works for rich locals here. Lawyers notarize forged documents and pretty well do as they please. Worse than that, many of them are connected to the thriving drug trade between here, Mexico and the US. Life is cheap. Gringos are regularly gunned down by hit men on motorcycles, right in this town. One minute you're having a quiet drink in a bar or walking on the street. Next thing, a motorcycle pulls alongside. The guy on the pillion looses of with an Uzi and you're history. Best forget the whole thing."

His glamorous realtor sold him a cheaper house and then was no longer friendly. The roof leaked when it rained. The promised internet connection was desperately slow and intermittent. To cap it all, the sugar cane field next door was burning and the smoke meant he had to stay indoors coughing.

A call to his friend the wildlife expert added to his misery. "Hi, how about we meet up in your favorite bar for a few beers? Maybe you could ask the girls around."

"Yeh look, I'm busy with visitors from Germany this week, but if you want an individual tour I could fit you in after next Thursday. It'll be only $300 a day for a returning customer."

* * *

Four years on, Albert had learnt a few painful lessons. The climate was indeed splendid in January and February. The rest of the year it alternated between months of steamy, leather-rotting tropical downpours and parched dry conditions. There was the windy season, the black fly season, the dust season and the cane field burning season and the seemingly endless wet season. The largest of several terrifying earthquakes had shattered the tiles on his floors. He could not afford to have them repaired.

Internet connectivity continued to be slow and regularly failed altogether. Due to this and the lack of face-to-face meetings, the expected income from his New York clients had virtually dried up.

Soon after he arrived he discovered that the hookers in the tourist bars were atypical of the general population of young women. Lack of exercise and a diet of sugary soda and Kentucky fried meant that most looked like wobbly caterpillars, clad in unflattering spandex, several sizes too small. Few of them spoke English. Even their Spanish was an incomprehensible local dialect. Most disliked fat old gringos with little Spanish and no manners. All the gringos did was complain about how much better things were in the US of A. 'Why didn't they go back there?'

A young local girl had moved in with him. She was far from a beauty, but the best he could get. When she kept demanding money and stealing things, he threw her out. Then he was hit with a lawsuit for palimony and had to buy her off from his rapidly dwindling savings.

Apart from drinking himself stupid with cheap rum on his mosquito-infested patio, he had no pleasures left. His house was plagued with scorpions. Poisonous snakes roamed the garden and there were flies everywhere. Things were desperate. He was about ready to pack it in. But what could he do?

Returning to the States was out. His wife was suing him for the rest of the divorce settlement, which he no longer had.

Then, out of the blue, a letter came from his sister in Rochdale, England. It was post-marked three months earlier.

Dear Albert,

I am sorry I have not been in touch earlier, but I have been rather busy here.

Since Father died, ten years ago, Mother has gradually faded away. She is in Rochdale Infirmary and is asking to see you. It is pancreatic cancer. They say she is unlikely to last another two weeks.

I know you have not kept in touch since that terrible row with Dad, but you need to come home. I expect she will be leaving the house to the two of us.

Do come as soon as you can. I miss you and really need your help and support.

Your loving sister,

Alice.

Suddenly, for the first time in years he could see a glimmer of hope.

He remembered his happy childhood summers in Rochdale, sailing his yacht on Syke Pond. He used to go fishing for sticklebacks in the canal with his pals. They caught the tiny fish with nets on bamboo sticks and kept them in jam jars. In the summers, they would ramble past the creepy ruins of haunted Clegg Hall and hike on across the moors. He recalled the rowing boats on Hollingworth Lake and the happy picnics, by the side of his dad's old Ford Anglia.

He thought of the expeditions to collect wild blackberries in the hedgerows or to go bilberrying on the moors. The family's tongues would turn purple from eating the ripe fruit. There were always berry pies and lots of jam following these trips.

The beatings his father gave his mother, the time he caught his drunken dad trying to rape Alice and his mother's stony-faced denials were memories suppressed in the deepest recesses of his brain. He only remembered the good times. He would go back to England. Things would be better.

* * *

A week later, he arrived at Manchester Airport on the cheapest possible flight, via Amsterdam. He was drained from the near twenty-four hours of travelling in cramped seats. The sandwiches tasted of soggy cardboard after sweating in their plastic film. A baby screamed in his ear for the whole flight. The boy in the next seat threw up over his jeans when they hit a long patch of bumpy turbulence.

As he cleared customs, he was shocked to see Alice after thirty years. Her hair was grey. She limped slowly with a stick. Her face was wrinkled and old. She had withered arthritic hands with liver spots.

She likely saw changes in him too. He was almost entirely bald, with a drinker's tremor, a sagging belly and haggard cheeks. He stank of vomit and sweat.

"Oh Albert. You look terrible. Let's get a cup of tea at the café. That usually helps."

He gave a hollow laugh, how English. When she went to the ladies room, he poured a hip flask of raw rum into his teacup and guzzled it down. The sting of it burned into his ulcer and he clutched his stomach.

* * *

He was shocked by his parent's house where Alice still lived. The small garden was overgrown with weeds. The paint was peeling from rotting window frames. Inside, the rooms seemed darker and much smaller than he remembered.

The place reeked of musty old people. Everything was worn, dull and Twenty years out of date. The springs in the easy chairs had gone. Stuffing poked through the worn upholstery on their arms.

The bronze statue of a runner that his dad had won back in the fifties in the Lancashire cross-country championships still stood on the dark wood of the sideboard. Albert had always hated it and all it stood for. He could hear his dad berating him. "Yer nowt but a little weed. When Ar were your age Ar were a champion runner."

* * *

Alice took him on a tour of the town. It was nothing like he remembered. The town hall was the only place he recognized, built in the grand gothic style by the mill owners during King Cotton's brief reign of prosperity. The sooty grime of the smog and smoke had been sand blasted away. The building was still majestic, a monument to men who valued civic pride above giving decent wages and housing to their workers.

His family's red brick council house in Belfield was still there. They had lived there before their parents bought a house of their own. The municipality developed the estate to provide homes fit for heroes after World War II. As such socialist experiments failed, the town council had sold off these properties. Now each had a different coloured door.

He reminded Alice. "Remember the houses used to all have the same blue doors in the proper egalitarian manner. Look! The arched entries through to the back gardens are still there. We used to kick balls to and fro in the tunnel.

"Remember. The coal men used to heave big sacks through the entry to the bunker out the back. Their faces and hands were always black with coal dust and a leather flap at the back of their hats protected their shoulders from the heavy sacks."

As they lingered to look at their old home, half a brick bounced of the car hood with a clunk, leaving a dent. Some Asian-looking youngsters appeared ready to toss more at them. "Hey Mister, watchya lookin' at? Whities not welcome here! This is our town."

They drove around the rest of the area at a faster pace. She showed him the various mosques. There was a big one with a blue dome and impressive minaret in Trafalgar Street. She remarked, "I'm surprised they haven't renamed it Mohamed Street. This town is run by and for the immigrants now."

They laid flowers by their parents' modest headstone in the cemetery. Whole sections were given over to the newcomers. The grave markers had no crosses and bore Asian scripts. Albert raised an eyebrow. "What would dad have said to all this? You know what a racist he was."

Alice told him, "We have to keep quiet now if we don't want trouble. There are lots of knifings and attacks on white people at night. It's best to stay indoors."

Ignoring her advice, Albert went looking for the old Victorian pubs he used to frequent. They had been full of tobacco smoke and men hawking into spittoons. They were all gone.

In the town centre, he found a pub in Toad Lane called The Baum. The beers he used to drink were all history. The prices of the new stuff were astronomic. He tried to strike up a conversation with some of the drinkers. There was a young couple at a nearby table. The man's arms were heavily tattooed. His jet-black hair was gelled into spikes and he wore an earring. The woman sported pink hair. She had a stud in her nose and flowers tattooed on her neck.

"I've been abroad for over thirty years. I hardly recognize this place with all the immigrants"

The man glowered at him, "Listen pal. No one cares about what things were like thirty years ago. The immigrants have as much right to be here as us. My mum's Romanian. Now clear off you fascist git!"

He staggered towards home, the worse for drink, through the litter-strewn streets and past spray-painted graffiti. A couple of muscular bruisers barred his path. They had accents which were a mixture of East European overlaid with Lancashire idioms and flat 'A's. "Give us yer money granddad!"

He tried to run past them, but they tripped him and kicked him unconscious.

* * *

The ambulance crew dumped him on a gurney in the casualty department. A doctor, who seemed to be from somewhere in Africa, gave him a cursory examination and a jab with some painkiller. Then Albert waited for hours, as more serious cases took precedence. It was a scene from Dante's Inferno.

An Irishman, who looked as if his bloodied head had been in a spin drier and who had an ear hanging off, was being questioned by harassed and over-worked young doctors. "Have you been drinking?"

"Oi drank ten pints o Guinness."

"What happened to you?"

"Oi can't remember."

Patients with stab wounds and a man who had been hit by a truck were all treated before Albert. Some drunks tried to fight the hospital staff and the police arrived to sort them out. He closed his eyes and waited his turn.

* * *

A week later, Albert was flat broke and his shattered ribs still tortured him with every breath. Alice told him, "Mother left the house to me in her will. The lawyer said mother felt it only right 'cos I looked after her all these years and you never even wrote."

The next morning it was raining heavily. When she arose, Alice found Albert long gone. His bed was cold.

He hitched a lift from a friendly Bulgarian truck driver. Albert persuaded the fellow to illegally drop him off on the hard shoulder of the M62 road which crosses the Pennines, the hills that form the spine of England.

The freezing low cloud partly hid him from passing traffic, as Albert trudged dejectedly to the center span of the highest bridge on the motorway. He heard a piercing siren as a police car rolled slowly up behind him. Glancing over his shoulder, he spotted two burly cops in orange visibility jackets fast approaching. Their car was parked behind them with its lights flashing. "Hoy you! Where the 'ell do ya think you're goin?"

Albert considered running onto the roadway in front of the headlights of the heavy trucks dimmed by the rain. He could almost feel the thump, as one would run him down. The cops rushed him from behind trying to catch his arm. He vaulted over the barrier and into the misty void below.

The End

RED RORY'S NIGHTMARES

Or
be careful what you wish for

"The Revolution devours its children"

Jacques Mallet du Pan

Rory Murphy awoke drenched in sweat at 4 am. Throwing back his sodden covers, he raised his head from the wet pillow to glance at the clock. "Oh shit! Not again."

He fell back in despair. Yet another restless night had left him still exhausted. As he tossed and turned trying to sleep, he found himself remembering scraps of his father's stories. "Son, we live in America, but never forget we are pure bred Irish, both on mine and your mother's side. Our people came over during the potato famine. It was leave or rot by the hedgerows. The boats were hell ships full of fever, dysentery and death. The damned English let us starve. Ever since, we've supported the struggles against those bastards."

Rory's thoughts wandered back to the classroom at St. Columba's school in New York. Father Brennan is taking the register, whilst the boys sit in cowed rows with feigned, rapt attention. The priest looks up sternly, as each boy responds. "Present Father."

He ticks off each child on his list, getting to the long string of Murphies. None of them are close relatives. "Aiden Murphy, Brendan Murphy, Declan Murphy, Fergal Murphy, Kieran Murphy, Liam Murphy, Malachy Murphy, Michael Murphy, Padraig Murphy, Rory Murphy."

Rory is thinking, *Jeez we Murphies must be great breeders.'*

He is jerked alert by the priest's snarling tone and glare. "Rory Morphy! Are ye asleep already boy?"

Rory dodges the wooden chalk eraser, as it hurtles within an inch of his head, clattering onto the floor. The priest glowers at him formulating a suitable bullying insult for this flame haired lad. He notices that Rory's has been cropped short. "Ye know what your hair reminds me of?"

He malevolently makes the class await his verbal blow. Then he delivers it with a smirk, as though it is the wittiest remark ever made. "A lavatory brush."

Some of the boys titter dutifully. As required, Rory returns the duster to Father Brennan's desk. Cowering, he tries to shrink his head into his shoulders. Cringing, he receives a sharp clip round his ear for his trouble. It stings like hell.

Now years later, he yearns to return to his slumbers, but memories of his father's lectures continue to intrude. "Murphies were with Wolfe Tone. We fought with pikes at the Boyne. One of yer grandda's brothers was shot without trial outside Dublin Post office in 1916. The friggin' English again!

"Dungarvan, where we come from, was a hotbed of revolt against the Black and Tans. Great uncle Seamus smuggled in tommy guns in his fishing smack. We Murphies did our bit all roit.

"We've always given generously to the Provos' and to the Kennedys' political funds. Never forget to support the fight against the Northern Prods for the rest of the lands that the Saxons stole."

Rory cannot get the dammed rebel songs out of his head. Snatches of 'By the Risin' of the Moon' are ruining his chances of getting back to sleep. And tomorrow, he is to march behind the pipe band and his father's former police precinct in the St Patrick's Day parade. *Da will be drunk before then. Ah well, the 17th is always a grand day.'*

* * *

Come daylight, through bleary, bloodshot eye-balls, he trims his fiery red beard in the bathroom mirror. His haggard reflection stares balefully back at him. He groans at the black shadows beneath his eyes. He really has to escape these recurrent nightmares.

Much of his spare time from teaching economics at Fordham is spent playing the rebel on the Internet. From the imagined safety of his home office, he loves the thrill of fomenting revolution using his pseudonyms. Sometimes, he forgets which alias and password he is using. Maybe that is what is driving him crazy.

He wonders what his dad would think, if he knew that his son's rebellious ideas are so much wider than a focus on tiny Ireland. *Dad is a great believer in the US Constitution, law and order and all that. What would he say if he thought I craved a new American revolution?'*

Rory enjoyed his trips to the romantic Emerald Isle, *'But it's so small and except to the Irish diaspora, insignificant. Besides it's always so friggin' wet.'*

His bookshelves are lined with histories of revolutions from the Spartacus Rebellion to the African Wars of Independence. He has an encyclopedic collection of revolutionary theoreticians and philosophers: Wildman, Tom Paine, Rousseau, Mao, Che and Regis Debray. He has read extensively about horrible violence, especially during the Great Terror of the French Revolution. His most troubling nightmares seem to have direct parallels with these events.

* * *

Nightmare 1 - Rory is a modern Rousseau. He has proposed new economic ideas to replace the already tried and failed Marxist Leninism of his more old fashioned comrades.

Due to the success of his bestselling book, 'The New Socialist Utopia', he has emerged from behind his aliases to claim the tome as his own. It has brought him the adulation of many women and street fighters. Serious thinkers now accept his formula for overthrowing the bankers, the big businesses and the elitist politicians. His supporters now believe in the violent installation of a better way. Sometimes, Rory thinks his work is just an excuse for mindless activists bent on anarchy. Mostly he prefers to thinks of it as giving them an ultimate goal to fight for.

During the current US revolution, his personal role in the street fighting had been bloody and successful. In public meetings he is cheered as a hero. He proudly wears the black patch over the eye which he lost to a National Guard rifle bullet during the storming of the Pentagon.

Morphing into a new Robespierre, he now sits daily in the commandeered Supreme Courtroom in Centre St, New York City. There, he chairs the Revolutionary Tribunal tasked with the summary liquidation of any opponents who survived the brutal street murders of a few weeks earlier.

The Revolutionary Council had sent him back to New York. They recognized the city as the nest of the moneymen, the real rulers of the old regime.

Drawing directly on French Revolutionary experience, justice in his court is swift and decisive. The accused are forbidden to speak. If they try, their mouths are duct-taped shut.

They are allowed no legal representation and cannot call witnesses. The five-person tribunal passes only one sentence, by simple majority. The last member who questioned Rory's proposed judgment quickly joined the guilty against the bloody, pock-marked wall outside. There, the barrels of the bucking machine guns run hot, as they shred those deemed guilty of exploiting the masses into a bloody pulp.

In the court the screaming, howling mob hurls abuse at the cringing and cowering bankers, CEOs and politicos during their trials. Others bellow their anger and mockery as they are dragged outside and bound to metal posts. Some of the convicted are so battered that they can no longer stand. As the months pass, ever more junior minions are dragged to the wall.

Rory has begun to have doubts, especially about the wives and older children. They all meet the same fate as their fathers and husbands. Younger kids are sent to Rikers for rehabilitation. Others are held in Sing Sing for execution later. Infants are fostered out to worthy rebels.

Halfway through an especially busy morning, the mob bursts into his courtroom. As he tries to shout for order, Rory is drowned out by shouts of "Death to the murderers!" and "Kill Murphy!"

For weeks, he has expected a reaction from opponents to the extremists, who he now leads. He remembers the fate of Danton and Robespierre, his childhood heroes. However, the suddenness of this outburst terrifies him. His stomach clenches. His heart races.

He leaps up looking wildly about, considering where he can run. A bullet slams into his shoulder. Then he is beaten unconscious by many fists. This must be death.

Next morning, he awakes in agony. Rough hands drag him into his own courtroom, battered and chained. Mary, his son Sean who is only twelve, and about twenty others, are already in the cage for the accused. He is tossed in and its iron door clangs shut. The room spins before him.

His untreated wound seeps blood. He clings to his trembling family. Through the slits of his swollen eyes, he sees that his wife and son are also badly bruised, their clothing torn and their faces and hands filthy and scarred.

He hardly hears much of their five-minute collective trial. His loved ones are torn from his arms. As he reaches out trying to protect them, a truncheon blow knocks him out.

He comes to outside. His head hurts like hell and is pumping blood from a further deep gash. His shattered jaw and broken teeth are throbbing.

Mary is bound to a post, wide eyed and screaming with terror. Sean and some other youngsters are tethered near her. The guns rattle and roar. He closes his eyes, venting a bloody, silent scream. As he is dragged forward, he loses control of his bladder.

Rory wakes shouting. Mary grumps at him. "Not again Rory. You'll have to sleep in the guest room from now on. I need my goddamn rest."

* * *

Nightmare 2 - Rory has tried to hide behind his on-line alias. He is living in a clapboard Cape Cod house in Tarrytown, up the Hudson River from New York.

He realizes he has been outed as the author of revolutionary books and blogs when TV news vans and many cars appear outside his house. As he answers the incessant ringing of the doorbell, reporters wielding furry microphones, cameras and large video recorders thrust them into his face. He is overwhelmed with the questions and blinded by the flashes. "Rory Murphy, you wrote, 'Massacre the Elites.' Have you anything to say to our viewers?"

"Rory! Look this way!"

"Do you really want to murder the rich and confiscate their property?"

"Do you expect to be arrested for proposing the slaughter of all those in government?"

"Are you just a commie?"

"Is it true they call you Red Rory?"

"Are the Chinese paying you?"

Panicked and confused, Rory finally heaves the door shut against the crush of bodies. He has to stab one foot with the point of a handy umbrella from by the door. He and Mary run around closing the curtains, as the paparazzi bang on the windows taking more photos. Terrified, little Sean hides under the stairs from the din.

Within minutes, police black and whites arrive, sirens screaming and red strobes rotating. They block off the street. Rory is already tossing a few things into a suitcase. He needs to get out, before FBI agents arrive to arrest him.

He climbs over the fence to a friendly neighbor's house. The sympathetic man spirits him away in the trunk of his car.

Rory makes a brief call from a phone booth. His hysterical wife tells him that the FBI is virtually taking the house apart. He ends the call as an agent tries to speak to him. "Rory, you'd best give yourself up quietly…"

He hides out in a motel. When he attempts to send a few messages from his computer using his aliases, some accounts no longer work. Others are full of messages from reporters. He disconnects in case the FBI traces his location.

As dusk approaches, a black van pulls up right outside his door. Peeping through the fisheye lens, he spies four people wearing shiny plastic Anonymous masks. They look sinister, so he keeps the door firmly shut and hooks the chain.

They kick the door in shattering the wood. Forcing a black hood over his head, the intruders bundle him into their van. Rough hands tie his hands with plastic cable ties. As he bounces around on the cold metal floor, he wonders what the hell is going on. He shouts questions. "Who are you? Where are we going? Why are you doing this?" There is no answer.

His captors take him to a safe house. The view from the barred windows suggests it might be in the Catskills. Security is tight. He spots guards with assault rifles and shotguns patrolling the grounds. Some hold fierce looking Dobermans straining at their leashes. Inside, the leader's face is hidden by a black balaclava.

The others treat the leader with great respect. He tells Rory, "You're a revolutionary icon now. This is the time for you to help us storm Washington."

"Hang on a minute. I'm just a theorist. I'm asthmatic and no street fighter."

"Professor, we need you. You'll be looked after. We'll start with the video."

A few days later, Rory is beginning to like his new role of celebrity revolutionary. A pretty blonde girl, of an age where she could have been his daughter, makes love to him with enthusiasm and apparent awe.

Later, he watches his performance on CNN. With powerful, slashing hand gestures, he speaks with fire, eyes flashing with passion. His distinctive red beard and hair really make him look the part. "Now is the time to strike back. We can't sit waiting to be slaughtered. For the future of our nation we must rise up now. Come to Washington. We will storm the citadel of corruption and burn it down!"

In the next days, his minders move him from place to place. He is no longer bound, but is always hooded. Sometimes, he travels in car trunks.

He hears the masked leader on a cell phone. "The President's already in bunker 7. The attack will go ahead. Destroying the buildings alone will get us enough media coverage to ignite the spark."

On the day of the big demonstration, Rory is getting cold feet. He has not heard from his family for over a week. His guards tell him they are safe, but he wonders.

He rides in the trunk of yet another vehicle and hears the roar of a crowd. Bullhorns lead the slow chanting. "Hey, Madam President, we want you!" The staccato response roars from thousands of throats. "Dead! Dead! Dead!"

He feels weakness in his knees at the crackle of distant gunfire. They have told him to wear the black wig and dark glasses until the moment of triumph. "You'll be kept safe till then."

His blonde guides him by the hand and looks at him adoringly. They are borne along in the swirling mass of placard-waving people. A man with a camcorder keeps sighting on him. He begins to relax. He has protection. He is in disguise. He is not near the front of what they told him was to be 'a peaceful demonstration'. The gunfire seems to have stopped. Maybe it was something else or perhaps rounds fired into the air.

He begins to join in the responses to the bull-horns with increasing enthusiasm, as they roll along with the flow. He catches the excitement of the moment. "Hey, you policemen, stop protecting your oppressors. Come and join us." "Now! Now! Now!"

He inhales that exhilarating feeling of crowds and collective action. His step lightens. His heart beats stronger. Nothing can stop this.

Suddenly, on a prearranged signal, the front ranks seem to file towards the rear. A man in an Anonymous mask, with a bullhorn shouts. "Now!"

Rory's wig and dark glasses are whisked away, revealing his bright red hair. Disoriented, he blinks at the sudden light. He feels hands pushing him forward.

Someone thrusts a gun into his hand. The man with the camera focuses on him. The crowd gives him space. He looks up and sees the three lines of troops pointing assault rifles with fixed bayonets at the mob. He cannot see their eyes behind their visors.

Four attack dogs are rushing towards him. Rory panics, aiming the gun and firing at the nearest one. He is cut down in a hail of lead. He feels no pain only warm relaxation. A voice, as if far away, says, "We have our martyr."

Rory sits bolt upright in his bed, dripping with sweat. "That must be the fifth time I've had that one."

* * *

The last nightmare - This one seems different. It is new. His subconscious mind hopes there will be a better ending. He dreams there is a call in the night. He is in his bed a home. The ring tones on his cell phone are persistent. Sleepily he mumbles, "Who is it?"

"Thank god I got you Rory."

He recognizes is the voice of a Jesuit priest friend from Fordham. He glances at the clock. "What the hell's wrong? It's two in the morning."

"You need to get out now! A sympathizer in the FBI just called. He says they're on the way to your house. You're wanted for treason."

"But I only write about it."

"Get out man!"

Adrenalin pumping, Rory leaps up. Throwing on a pair of jeans, a T-shirt, a hooded track jacket and Reeboks, he rushes towards the stairs. Rheumy eyed, Mary opens her bedroom door. "Rory, you've set off the alarm. What's goin' on?"

"I've to get out. The FBI are comin' for me."

As he sprints from the house, there are roaring engines and fast approaching headlights. He dashes into the nearby wood and immediately stumbles over a fallen tree, cracking his knee against a stone. He staggers on, limping painfully.

Eventually he makes it to the back of the Rockefeller estate where he often walks. He never pays the entrance fee. The rich Rockefellers still live all over the estate. Why should he support them?

He wriggles through the familiar gap in the chain-link fence. His knee has swollen and hurts. Shivering with cold, he falls again. Thorns tear at his hands and legs.

At last, he can't hear any pursuit. All in, he slumps beneath a tree. It is freezing and he tugs up the hood of the jacket, pulling the sleeves over his bleeding fingers. He slips into a troubled slumber.

With the first light of dawn, the crack of a twig wakes him. His hands are numb with cold. He sees the frost on the ground around him. He just wants to go back to sleep.

Then he hears the excited yelping of hounds on the scent. He starts to run. *'Wait! Is this a dream? It seems too real.'*

He puts a foot into a rabbit hole, falling and banging his head. He touches the bruise and feels blood seeping between his fingers. A slavering wild-eyed dog sinks its teeth into his leg. Other dogs grab on to him, growling. He screams. *'This has to be real.'*

A big man in a bulletproof vest and FBI cap bursts through the trees and then another. "Is it Red Rory?"

"Yep."

They take up the standard two-handed shooting stance. He sees the black holes in the barrels of their guns. They fire.

The end

I LUST THEREFORE I AM - UN CRIME PASSIONNEL

"Lust is to the other passions what the nervous fluid is to life; it supports them all, lends strength to them all. Ambition, cruelty, avarice, revenge are all founded on lust."

Donatien Alphonse François, Marquis de Sade

Jacques considered his plight as he watched the clouds slowly passing below the aircraft's window. He had led as dissolute a life as any Frenchman could. He regretted none of it. His only wish was that he had had even more affairs with his employees', suppliers' and friends' wives and daughters. Sadly, all that seemed no longer possible.

Throughout his privileged life as the heir to a large chateau and several wineries, he had feasted copiously on the best cuisine in the world. His girth reflected this. He sported a well-stuffed stomach, lived-in face, nose with broken red veins and bleary eyes. Now, he was sad that there would be no more gourmandizing.

He had always appreciated the subtle aromas, delicious after-tastes and intoxicating properties of fine wines, especially the premiers crus from his own Aloxe-Corton Chateau. His taste buds and olfactory senses were tuned like a Stradivarius. The simple pleasures of the grape were about to end.

The jolting stiletto stabs in his joints and debilitating aches in his various bones and muscles were beyond endurance. They had escalated in frequency and intensity over recent months, as if his body was vengefully seeking to consume itself with dozens of sharp knives and forks as retribution for its abuse.

He could no longer even give the famous Gallic shrug without wincing in torment through gritted teeth. For a Frenchman, this severely limited both the joy and extent of conversation.

So, he had decided to bring his life to its conclusion. Well, c'est la vie, or rather the opposite.

His tolerant and long-suffering wife, Giselle, sat in the aisle seat. She looked lovingly at him and remembered their early days. She had married him when her father owned an adjoining vineyard and Jacques was a dashingly debonair member of the National Gendarmerie Intervention Group, GIGN. He had looked so handsome in his kepi and captain's dress uniform, proudly displaying his Legion d'Honneur. He had won this for secret acts of bravery in fighting terrorists in Africa. She knew little of the details, but to her he was a fascinating James Bond type, full of mystery and élan.

Of course, she had admired this handsome youth from a distance, even as a child. He was a few years older so he never seemed to notice her. She had held him in awe as he led gangs of his playmates in noisy games of pirates, Gauls against the Romans and endless boisterous mischief.

Often, she had listened to her parents tut-tutting at his latest exploits, commenting. "That boy will end up guillotined or in prison one day." To her, he seemed a young Napoleon, exciting her pubescent hormones and bringing sweet dreams of unending romantic love.

On the plane and incessantly before that, she assured him that his current afflictions were the wages of sin. She clung to her Roman Catholic ideas of divine retribution in the forlorn hope that he might yet change. His stubbornness made her blood boil, but every time she was about to explode with anger she calmed herself with a prayer that one day he should repent.

In the past, her comments would have amused him. Today, her insistence on linking his crippling and ever more excruciating joint and muscular pains to his lifestyle, just made him angry. It was as if she wanted him to suffer. He hated her when she was like this.

The illness had struck him down like a lightning bolt. One day he was a fairly fit and active man of 68, looking forward to another ten years of debauchery, the next he could hardly move. Most nights were endless purgatories of sweat-soaked agony. Between spasms, he contemplated various methods of suicide.

Giselle refused to even entertain his idea of a euthanasia clinic in Switzerland. "Only God can take our lives. Our Church cannot condone suicide." She longed for him to return to Holy Mother the Church, even if it were to be a deathbed repentance.

He felt his wish to end it all was perfectly reasonable. So be it. He would act without her help. He considered some options. *Maybe I could loop a light wire hawser around a tree and tie it securely. Then I would pass it through the driver's window of my Peugeot, looping a noose for my neck. I'd have to leave it all nice and slack, so then I could then push it through the opposite window and tie it off round another tree.*

Next, I would climb into the driver's seat and slip the wire noose over my head. Starting the engine and holding the car on the footbrake to build up the revs, I would release the brake and hit the gas. With a mighty roar and smoking wheels, I am neatly decapitated. All the mess is contained in the vehicle. Perfect!

'If it were done on the edge of the old quarry on my estate and I ensured that the cigar lighter was hot enough to detonate the fuel tank with a satisfying Kaboom!, there would only be charred remains. Giselle need not suffer too much. I still love the silly old thing.

'Mmm, I don't think I can do all that in my present condition. Scrambling in and around the car would hurt too much and I'm not limber enough with all this stiffness and pain from every movement.

'Maybe my old, special forces Manhurin revolver would be easier.' He smiled, remembering how he dispatched two terrorists in an alley in Abidjan. Both were perfect double taps, one shot to the torso and one to the head, exactly as they had trained him in the Special Force's "death house". *'It was the biggest adrenaline rush of my life. Kill*

or be killed. One of the guys was unarmed and trying to surrender. I should have taken him in for questioning, but my blood lust was up.

'I still love the heavy, blued steel of the gun. Its heft is perfect in my hand. Giselle thinks I was a hero, but I was a complete bastard and enjoyed every minute of it. Every young Frenchman should be allowed to slaughter Arabs. It's our historic right and destiny. Marie Le Pen understands.

'I insert the barrel into my mouth and bang! The hollow point ammunition blows off the back of my skull. All pain stops. Voila!'

Giselle was relentlessly opposed whenever he mentioned his desire to end it all, even though he kept the details to himself. Last time she had said. "Think of me. What about our daughters? They love you. Maybe we can find a cure for you? Stop drinking, chasing women and eating so much and maybe you'll get better."

"I might as well be dead!" was his angry retort, but arguing did no good. She had tolerated his gross behavior and suffered every indignity and infidelity because she still loved him, all 120 kilos of his louche, bull headed masculinity. *'Maybe it was her religion that kept her in line. Suffering on earth led to rewards in heaven. Ha ha!'*

He noted a passing cloud, then continued his reverie. *'As soon as they returned to Burgundy, he would act. One of his workers would dig a shallow hole in the vineyard. Standing on the edge, he would pull the trigger. Bang! No fuss, no mess. His last view would be of the ripening grapes and his beloved chateau, a fitting end to a splendidly dissolute life.'*

At least the flights were going to plan. Giselle had arranged for a wheel chair transfer through Madrid airport. On the Iberia flight from Panama he ate a hearty dinner of excellent Spanish food. Each course was delivered with wines, perfectly chosen by the airline's sommeliers. A generous glass of Tio Pepe accompanied the marcona almonds and olives he loved so much. He delighted in the freshness, fruity and young, of the Pazo San Mauro Albariño 2014. The robust red of the El Vínculo Reserva 2010 went exactly with the suckling pig. Everything was cooked to perfection and artistically presented.

Jacques savored every mouthful with his eyes closed, tuning out his own pain and Giselle's exhortations not to have any more wine. If he was on his way to death, he was at least determined to enjoy a condemned man's last meal or three. He looked forward to some decent French food after all the Latin American rubbish of recent weeks. At least Iberia got it right.

He ploughed on through the sweet richness of the dessert, relishing a large glass of Cardenal Cisneros, Jerez Pedro Ximenéz. Finally, a double Gran Duque de Alba licor de brandy with his coffee transported him into a fitful doze.

He jerked awake. The plane was about to land in Madrid. Even the flat bed seat had tormented his slumbers. He felt as if he'd been sleeping on rocks. There had been no position in which he could arrange his aching limbs to give him any relief. He had a skull-splitting hangover, could hardly move his tortured legs to get to the bathroom and had Giselle complaining, "I told you so."

He threw her a malevolent glare. *'If only I had the gun here, I'd end it right now and maybe her first.'*

Despite the pains, he was impressed by the way the airline managed the wheel chair transfers. He had often seen disabled passengers at airports, without giving much thought to the process. They tended to get in his way. The attendants expected precedence and used the chairs like bulldozers.

His attendant whisked him passed the long lines at immigration control. Jacques' entry to the EU was stamped into his passport tout suite. He began wheeling Jacques towards the first class lounge to await the transfer to his next flight.

Meantime, Giselle was indulging herself in last minute shopping in the upscale airport shops. *'As if the five extra bags she had already checked through were insufficient.'*

Jacques smiled grimly. Soon he would need to suffer no further shopping trips nor, what was even worse, listen to her irritating complaints and intricate details about every purchase. What did he care about whether a shop assistant was surly, or what color blouse Giselle bought.

Jacques' pangs eased a little as his chair was maneuvered like a barracuda through a shoal of baitfish. Despite his aches, he began to realize the advantages of wheelchair travel. Security searches were perfunctory. People gave way as the chair barged its way to the front of any line. Instead of suspicious and resentful glares from uniformed officials, they were solicitous. He received looks of sympathy or maybe pity. The pretty douanière was really sexy and smiled when he said she looked cute.

Best of all though was the unexpected view from the lowly perspective of the chair. It was exactly at buttock height. He noted the many callipygous girls jiggling and wiggling ahead of him. They were off on holiday or looking into the fashion shops. They wore chic, loose but figure-hugging fabrics oblivious to anything else. Bliss!

He was positioned so that they could not see him ogling their derrieres. Even if they could, he was just a harmless old cripple. '*Ha!*'

His transport weaved smoothly through the crowds and the well-lit glitz of the duty free area, with its enticing displays of liquors, cosmetics and electronics. He was awfully tempted to reach out and grab a bottle of scotch. Even better, he might sample some of the young flesh sashaying before him.

He suppressed the urge, '*Best not. After all, I'm not in France yet. There, such things are better understood.*'

* * *

Next day, he woke in his own bed, rested and relieved. The splendid French doctor had sedated him. The torments were gone, at least for now. He tried a few faltering steps. The discomfort was there, but bearable. He leered at his reflection in the bathroom mirror. Maybe there were a few years of sinning left in this old goat yet.

After few days' rest, he felt well enough to return to his office at the winery. He hobbled through the door with a cane. For extra support, he slipped his hand round the firm young waist of his secretary and mistress Marie Claude. He let his hand grope lower as she closed the office door. Giggling, she helped him into his leather, high backed chair.

* * *

On their return, Giselle was puzzled by her maid's absence from work. The girl's mother had called saying she was ill, but was evasive as to what exactly her illness was.

Today, after a trip in her Citroen to the farmers' market in the village, her maid met Giselle at the door of the chateau. The girl was obviously pregnant and could not hold back her tears. "Come child," said Giselle, "tell me all about it."

Her maid blurted out the whole sordid story between sobs. Giselle felt bile rising in her stomach. It was a horrible story. The maid's father owed Jacques some money. The master blackmailed her into giving him sexual favors, often when Giselle was visiting her mother in Beaune. The girl wept as she told Giselle that Jacques liked to slap her about and humiliate her. This was too much.

As Giselle listened her fury grew. She could hardly blame the girl. Jacques was some kind of monster sent by the devil to torment her. All the pent up emotion of years suddenly burst into her brain like a thunderstorm. Something snapped in her head. A red veil blurred her vision and flushed her face. Incandescent with rage, she slipped something from a drawer into her handbag and seized the frightened girl by the hand.

Dragging her to the Citroen, she pushed her into the passenger seat. The car roared wildly along the twisting country roads. The tires screamed as Giselle fishtailed round corners. A local peasant leapt into a ditch for his life. She did not even notice him.

The maid clung desperately to the door handle, wide-eyed in sheer terror. Without stopping at the factory entrance, the car's front wing clipped the gatepost with a rending of metal. Finally they screeched to a halt in a shower of gravel, at the entrance to Jacques' office building.

When Giselle burst into view, the secretary tried to step forward but Giselle brushed past her, dragging the frightened maid along by the arm.

Giselle erupted into Jacques' office, shoving the pregnant girl forward. Jacques looked up puzzled. His eyebrows shot up when he saw the girl's swollen belly. His attempted smile froze as he noticed Giselle's crazed glare.

She shrieked "Monstre!" and hurled herself at him in a frenzied blur. The light glinted on something in her hand.

"Non Giselle!"

There was a sharp crack! crack! from her small automatic, as she emptied it into him. The first bullet grew in slow motion, as it streaked towards him. It smashed straight into his right eye. White light. Blackness.

The End

Gone but not forgotten–
A largely mythical state

"True friends stab you in the front."

Oscar Wilde

Bernard sits on their patio with his long-term partner, Jane, and their neighbours. Relaxing in their Adirondack chairs, they languidly sip iced daiquiris in the balmy air. The red ball of the sun is mesmerizing as it slides slowly below the far, jungle-clad mountains. Its passing paints the entire sky with fingers of fiery red, orange and pink. This flaming panorama is layered up to the highest wispy clouds. The silhouetted needle tufts of nearby pines add their own jet-black beauty.

As they savour the heavy scents of the honey-suckle and flowering tobacco, they all agree that it is yet another perfect tropical sunset. Alan gulps a fortifying mouthful from his cocktail and looks nervously at his wife Ann. Bernard and Jane sit forward expectantly. Alan's face seems to be sweating. His whole body seems rigid with tension. "We've been wanting to tell you something."

The hosts set down their drinks and focus their attention, wondering what on earth can be the matter.

"We've decided to move back to Chicago." Alan's following words come in a flood of released angst. "Ann wants to be near her grandchildren, especially the new baby. My parents are frail and we have to be closer to them. You are our best friends here. We wanted you to be the first to hear."

Bernard feels the muscles tightening in the pit of his stomach. He glances at Jane, thinking, 'She looks as though her face has been slapped.'

He forces a smile, while he formulates a response. "Well Ann, we've known that your daughter needs help with the new baby and they have been reluctant to schlepp down here to see you. As long as you are happy, that's the main thing. When is this due to happen?"

Ann replies, looking relieved. "Well I'm leaving next week. Alan will stay here to terminate the rental and pack up our stuff. We think in about a month we'll both be enjoying the frigid Chicago winter."

"Wow! That's fast." Jane says, recovering her composure and failing to laugh at the feeble attempt at levity about the weather. She thinks, 'They obviously decided this some time ago.'

The bombshell announcement puts a complete damper on the evening. Stumped for other words, Bernard and Jane make the usual instant platitudes about how they will be sorely missed, how Ann and Allen will always be welcome guests. Allen responds, "And you two can drop by Chicago each year on the way to see your friends in New York."

Shortly afterwards and earlier than usual, the friends leave. Everyone puts a brave face on it, with hugs and kisses all round. Ann and Alan set off on the short drive to their house on the next ridge.

As the electric security gate clicks behind them, Bernard takes Jane's hand, gently leading her back onto the patio. The sun has set, so he turns the floodlights on in the garden. He pours Jane another daiquiri and a stiff scotch for himself. Slumping in his chair he exclaims, "Shit! That's bad news."

Alan is Bernard's best friend, the most respected contributor at meetings of his favourite writers' group and his long-time bridge partner. Ann plays mah-jong with Jane. All of them are active members of the birding club.

They have other amigos and several dozen acquaintances. However this will surely leave a huge gap in their retirement life in their dream tropical paradise of Costa Rica's Central Valley.

Jane looks blankly at the garden for a while. "Well we thought this might happen and I'm sure it's what's best for them."

"You're right, we shouldn't be selfish, but a pattern seems to be emerging. People arrive; make new friendships in our slightly over friendly expat community, then they leave after a few years or in some instances within months."

They sit in silence for few more moments, distractedly regarding their hydrangeas and canna lilies, picked out by the lights. Bernard considers the bad news.

As a student, back in '69, he read a Russian short story. Maybe it was by Gogol, but perhaps not. Last time he tried to research Gogol on the Internet, Google insisted on substituting Gogol with its own name at every attempt.

He shares his thoughts with Jane. Gogol's tale is about some dead people buried in a graveyard. They have dwindling vestiges of mental activity. They can hear one another beneath the damp and wormy earth. Slowly, an Alzheimer's-like destruction occurs in their brains. Finally, they can only croak 'babok', like a group of fading frogs, until that too ceases.

"Jeez Bernie, that's awful gloomy." Jane contributes that their own experience demonstrates the impermanence of good neighbors. In every continent and country they have lived, humanity is transient. "People move to a place for many reasons: work, climate, culture, adventure, early retirement and eventually for care homes and death." She laughs uneasily at the last thought.

Engrossed in their somber dialogue, they look intently at one another. He gently squeezes her hand as they share ideas. For once they fail to notice the night turning chilly and a mist dimming the lights in the valley far below. Its clammy fingers crawl slowly up the mountain towards them.

They discuss why people move on. They quit for health reasons, bereavement or disappointment in the location. The endless torrential rain in October is depressing. So are the car wheel-shattering potholes. Other reasons are: poverty, the increasing incidence of robbery or a need to be near family members, old or young, in need of care. The reasons are many and compelling in every case.

He reminds her that many friends have faced the nightmare of one partner wanting to leave and the other not. Some couples weather this pulling-in-opposite-directions. In other cases relationships have ended in acrimony. In every situation, one or both parties left only after much wrangling and soul searching.

Jane opined that long timers could end up stranded. Maybe they foolishly put all their eggs into one, local financial basket. A few were on the run from dark lives elsewhere. Others stay because they bond with the locals, marry or find a viable career. Some simply have no better place to go in a hostile and troublesome world.

Bernard says, "When Alice was leaving, she told us that the neighboring Ticos all came to say how sad they were. Who knows whether these locals meant it, but at least they were polite."

With a cynically wry smile, Jane chuckles, "Mmm, maybe they were worried about the loss of yard and odd job work? Our part-time housekeeper tells me that she lives in fear of her other families moving on. Only last week, she said that costs here are getting so high and break-ins so frequent that she expects more of us to leave. Remember we've heard of several employees stealing things when they heard people are leaving. Others fleeced them by telling lies in the labor courts."

Jane voices her darkest concerns. "There's no perfect place, but do we really want to be that strange old man and woman, living in the weird old house that no one ever visits. Waves of younger and eager immigrants arrive full of hope. They fill the gaps the others leave. Many arrivals seem naïve and less interesting. Some stayers may become socially isolated. Could that happen to us?"

He pats her hand reassuringly and tries to look cheerful. "There are lots of ways for long timers to survive. Becoming the center of a social circle is one. Some of your women friends do that well. Think of the arts circle. It keeps them in touch with the incomers. Supporting charities, joining expat political groups and attending the computer club all have their devotees."

He snorts derisively. "Otherwise, it's smoking dope; drinking yourself into oblivion; jigsaws or reading."

A little to her dismay, he sets off on one of his analytical monologues. "The timing of transit waves depends on the state of the economy. In boom times, houses sell easily, in recessions they don't.

"Those who leave fondly imagine that old acquaintances will stay much as before. Facebook friends will be in regular touch. They will ask them to visit and stay with them. They will be made welcome. That's often an illusion. Cost and distance add to the difficulty of spending time together. New friends and new lives beckon."

Jane loves Bernie for his confident insights, but he can be a bit much. She decides to indulge him as he is at least talking sense.

He continues his monologue, blissfully unaware of her thoughts. "Some who remain, unconsciously see the leavers as destroyers of their dreams. They resent being abandoned. It seems that those who are leaving rank their fellowship lower than the siren calls of the new location. Remember this happened to us when we left Chicago?"

She adds, "Yes, I remember one neighbor. He was always so friendly, but he more or less told us there was no point in having us round in the last few months, as we would soon be gone." She looks wistful, "and I'd always thought his wife was a close friend."

Bernard mistakenly thinks she wants him to say more. "Departures pour cold water on our delusions of permanence. Each person leaving is unsettling to the dreams of those who remain. We all question our own decisions and reasons for being here.

"Too many of those we are friendly with here are really 'frenemies'. We don't actually like each other, but we need to be on hugs and kisses terms or we miss out on the local party scene. Behind our backs they badmouth us just as they do everyone else. I shan't miss those horrible types. Sadly, they are often the ones that stay the longest. Maybe they are unwelcome elsewhere.

"Only really close friends remain in touch across the years and continents. First it's weekly, then occasionally, 'babok'. Finally, it becomes holidays, 'babok'. Fortunately, we have many lifetime friends on five continents, but with others it's 'babok, babok, babok.'"

They go to bed and cuddle for reassurance and comfort.

✳ ✳ ✳

The next day Alan calls a temporary halt to the pool game and petty gambling at the weekly social gathering in the church hall. He stands and addresses everyone in a loud voice. "I have an announcement to make. Ann and I are going back to Chicago very soon."

As he gives their reasons, he becomes upset, as few appear to be listening any further. He hears one of the gamblers say, "I bid five." Then there is a clack of pool balls.

Frustrated, he regains some interest when he says, "I've brought a list of things we need to sell: the car, a fridge, the dehumidifier…"

Folk drift back to their games and largely ignore him for the rest of the session. The one or two exceptions sidle up like vultures for items on the list. "Is the fridge still available? Put me down for it."

* * *

The same evening Ann and Alan go to a party by a well-known local hostess. As usual, the food is a mish mash of easy-to-make American cuisine, mostly provided by the guests. The wine is the cheapest available and comes in boxes.

This time, Ann makes the announcement. Those who don't have their faces in the trough or were not at the church hall that morning, listen. Then, they return to their conversations. Some take selfies in front of the food or with their usual friends for their Facebook entries. One or two say how sorry they are. Ann is distressed at the almost total lack of interest.

For the rest of the party Alan and Ann feel like ghosts. People who normally chat to them slink away as they approach, as if they are suddenly invisible. Others do not make space for them to join their groups. They are shut out, shunned.

They leave sad and early with a few perfunctory 'Goodbyes'. Ann is mortified, "We've become 'other'!"

Alan puts a comforting arm round her shoulder as they walk home. "Well, look on the bright side. At least we have buyers for some of our stuff. We've learned the shallowness of some so-called friendships and we can leave with fewer regrets.

"Our best friends here, Bernie and Jane, will stay in touch. At least I hope so."

Ann bursts in to tears. "I hope so too, but what if they don't? I've a hole in my heart. I'll tell you this. I'm never coming back here!"

He produces a tissue. "I feel exactly the same, but remember that women make new close friends quicker than men. Hey! In Chicago, we can build new relationships. There are decent museums and cultural events every week with everything in English. The roads are much better too. We'll get ObamaCare, now that we are retirement age, as long as the Republicans don't close it down. The hell with this place!"

She smiles, as he reaches for her. From the strength and comfort of his arms, she looks up into his face. "Yes, but at least let's keep our many happy memories: astonishing sunsets, abundant and colorful wildlife, parties, spectacular hikes and those friends we will keep. Even friendships where we lose touch are worth remembering. They added value to our lives."

She rests her head against the warmth of his chest, as he says, "I really love you. Home for me will always be wherever you are."

The End

Passing it on

"Misery loves company"

John Ray

Bolted to a stout metal frame, next to two eleva-
tors that surface and dive deep into the vastness
of the underground car park, are set three plastic
seats. Tired from limping round the enormous
supermarket, James drops dejectedly into one of
them. His view of the aisles nearest the supermarket entrance is restricted, but he is focused
on his thoughts.

Feeling sorry for himself, he is hemmed in by
a large Coca Cola machine. Its red metal bulk
is intended to be a cheery enticement to buy its

toxic cans of chemicals and sugar but it also obscures his view of the endless row of checkouts. Though empty, the two neighbouring grey seats seem to push close. They pose a threat to his sore left arm and swollen knee.

He lets his head fall into his hands, wincing as the movement twists the inflamed muscles in his neck. His leg throbs as he bends it. Knives seem to be jabbing into the bones of his right foot. He sits with his eyes slitted against the brightness of the massive sales space, his forehead wrinkled with worry. At least there will be a few moments of relief from endlessly trailing his wife's trolley around the superstore.

She seemed determined to read every food label and consider each of the thousands of gaudily presented items in the place. James knows she is a loving person, seeking the best foods for them both and that she is concerned about his suffering. It was his grouchiness that led him to complain and then angrily leave her to it. *I'm always such a selfish bastard.'*

He feels a jolt in the seat and a corresponding twinge in his leg. He looks up to see a young, African-looking fellow, maybe a Somali, occupying the furthest chair. The man dumps a weighty cardboard box on the middle seat.

Totally absorbed in his own life bubble, the newcomer pulls out his mobile phone and begins an exuberant conversation in an unrecognizable language. Animatedly, he waves his arms to emphasize his points to an unseeing person far away.

Young people, mostly deep in cell phone chatter or texting, stroll past as they enter the store. They have so much vigour and energy. Some of the women have a sexy bounce, failing to register his presence and his following eyes. He recognizes that he is years beyond being of interest to the likes of them. Just as well, he had caused his wife enough grief the last time he'd had an affair some years back.

More slowly, old couples or singles stumble by. Some are pushed in wheel chairs. A wizened old woman, nearly bent double with age, takes tiny, faltering steps, leaning hard on her cane.

A careworn couple shepherds a lumpish, mentally handicapped son along. He is in his twenties, a burden for life, grimacing at passing shoppers and making loud grunts. This causes others to clear a wide path. James is sorry for them, but returns to musing on the dubious joys of his own inexorable decrepitude.

He is jerked from his melancholy by an old lady with a large shopping trolley. "Can I squeeze in?"

Without breaking his conversation, the Somali obligingly stands up, moving his parcel onto the vacated chair. James quickly shifts his left arm and knee, as the woman's enormous buttocks descend into the neighbouring seat, threatening to jar his sore limbs. The three connected chairs wobble with the impact as she settles in.

They sit in silence for a moment. James notices that she must be at least ten years older than him. Her trolley appears to have some special stability, allowing her to use it like a zimmer frame. He feels obliged to say, "It's good to get a rest. This place is far too big. I see that some people have those electric mobility scooters to help them get around."

"Yes I have one of those, but some of the smaller shops don't have enough room for the scooter so you have to clamber out before you can go inside. Getting in and out of the thing is the hardest part. So what's the point?"

"Oh, I'd never thought of that."

She produces a small polypropylene bottle of the dreaded Coke from her bag. "Do you think you could open this? It's too tight for me."

He takes it, wondering whether the soreness in the base of his thumb will allow him to grip it strongly enough. Fortunately, it twists off without much pain, leaving his sense of masculinity intact. "Yes they make everything too tight. There you go."

She sips a little cola. Unexpectedly, based on the tenuous link of his helping her, she launches into her weary tale. "Two years ago my husband had a prostate operation. It really made him miserable.

We'd been married for fifty years and he changed completely."

Sorry for her, he turns his head, tries to look sympathetic and softens his voice. "Oh dear, I know quite a few people who have had that condition. It brings traumatic changes and suffering." He is about to tell her of the recovery of friends to a semblance of normality, but she ploughs on.

"Yes he couldn't accept it. We used to like dancing and country walks. He was always the life and soul of the party. He hated the catheter he needed and had to empty the bag around his ankle every hour."

James sees that behind her glasses, her eyes are red from crying. He thinks, *'Poor woman, she must be desperate for someone to talk to if she's willing to share these intimacies with a stranger. I guess there are always people worse off than we are.'*

Her anguish pours out. "Two weeks ago, he left the house and they found him at the bottom of a bridge. It was terrible. A policeman knocked on our door with the news. I had to attend the inquest."

In shock at how grim this account has become, James struggles for something to say, his pains forgotten. He only manages a trite and wholly inadequate, "Oh how awful for you! I'm so sorry."

Her voice trembles a little. "He was seventy-nine. They said he pulled an empty trash bin onto the bridge and climbed on it to get up and over the railing. The coroner's verdict was suicide."

She seems surprised by the ruling. It makes sense to James, but he realizes she is in a state of confusion, poor dear.

"He used to pay all the bills. I never dealt with banks and credit cards. Now, I don't know what to do about everything."

Concerned, James asks her whether any relatives are around to help her. Wistfully, she says, "My son lives a hundred miles away in Kent. We don't see each other much because it's so far, but he came up for the inquest and the funeral."

Aware that it is a question that might elicit more distress, but might just help, James gambles. "Do you have grandchildren?"

"Yes, my grandson is a doctor in Canterbury."

He attempts to lighten a hopelessly depressing conversation. He thinks of his own nieces who are dedicated young doctors, devoted to the well-being of others. "He must be very clever to have studied to be a doctor. Very few succeed in getting that qualification."

"Yes, but I don't see him much either. It's a busy job. If I phone him to say I have a sore toe, he tells me to go to the doctor."

They sit in silence for a few moments. James wracks his brains for something else he might say to cheer her. There is nothing. His heart is in his boots with sorrow for the poor woman. He yearns to give her the hug she so badly needs, but that is alien to the British culture they both come from.

Deeply depressed, he thinks about his own future. Finally, he gives up saying, "Ah well, I'd best go find my wife."

As he struggles back to his feet his pains return. He sees a young woman taking his vacant seat and the older woman speaking to her. *'Poor girl, she is about to hear the same sad story. The old woman needs to tell people. I doubt if it can do much to help. Perhaps talking is cathartic.'*

James staggers a few steps forward as his stiff legs resume some semblance of walking. He winces at the renewed hurt. He looks left and right, pondering which direction to follow.

Out of the store and to the left, he might find a bridge that he could jump from onto the road below. What if he were to hit a passing car? The distress and psychological shock for the driver would be horrible. What if there were children in the car? What if someone were injured?

A deep lock on the nearby canal could do the trick. Drowning would be dark and cold at first, but he remembered the seductive warmth from a bathing incident as a child. He vividly recalled that after the lung-searing pain of breathing in the water, he had felt a serenity and peaceful warmth. Then the lifeguard had pounded his chest back into life and he had coughed up water. *'That hurt too. You have to do it right. How to avoid being unsuccessful? Tying a stone round my neck maybe?'*

What of his wife? He loves her. Unlike the lady in the next seat, she is the one who manages their finances and bills. She is strong. Does she need him? He is becoming a burden to her.

She might blame herself. How would she feel? Should he go back into the sales area to find her? If he were not there, no one would help put the groceries onto the checkout conveyor.

His suffering joints seem to be dragging him towards the floor. His heart is already down in his shoes. He reaches a decision. He turns and takes the first lurching step forward.

The End

THE CALL OF WHAT'S LEFT OF THE WILD - IT'S A DOG'S LIFE.

"He had killed man, the noblest game of all, and he had killed in the face of the law of club and fang"

Jack London, *The Call of the Wild*

The newborn German Shepherd is a cute little puppy, with big paws. He has only just opened his eyes. He suckles happily away alongside the comforting warmth of his siblings. The milky warm nipple is so comforting between his gums.

With grunts and whimpers, he begins to communicate with his big and cuddly milk supplier. She teaches him the beginnings of the language known only to dogs. She is surprised and pleased with him. This one, special among the others and all her previous litters, learns so rapidly.

He looks adoringly into her eyes, as she tells him what is in store and how to behave to best survive. "You're lucky not to be born into a breed that's damaged. See, in the next cage there are dogs with so much hair in their faces that they can't see well. Across the room there are some dogs that can't breathe properly because their muzzles are too short."

He hears them wheezing and sniffs their scent. Every nuance of smell tells him something. He can tell that few dogs around him are happy.

She knows she has to be quick, as they will have all too little time together. Indeed, his siblings are torn away one by one, in great distress. Their mother barks pathetically to no avail. "It's too early. They need my milk."

She slumps into silence, putting a protective paw over him; the last of her loved ones. She understands a little of human talk, but has long since realized that their merciless masters cannot understand dogs. The humans misinterpret dogs' fawning behavior to gain benefits as genuine love for them.

His mom tells the pup she hopes he will go to someone who will feed him well and look after him. "Maybe it'll be one of the foreign residents rather than the locals. Many of those are meaner and treat dogs badly."

He is terrified and clings to her, whimpering in his dreams. Next morning a family of gringos appears, two big ones with two young. They smile and make soft noises. They stroke him behind his ears. He likes that.

Then to his utter horror, they wrench him away from his protesting mother. He hadn't understood why they had said how cute he was. Forever afterwards, he will associate their deceptive smiles as an evil portent of dire events.

* * *

One of the small humans holds him tight as they climb into a huge red machine. The people smell disgusting. The machine reeks of a strange dog, nasty chemicals and oils. He wrinkles his nose in distaste. The mechanical monster makes strange rumbling noises and moves off.

They arrive at an enormous black gate. It whirrs open. A large fat dog rushes to greet them, wagging his tail. This dog has the same smell he remembers from the car. The big female pats this dog on the head. She says something he does not understand and calls the dog 'Dennis'.

Later, Dennis tells him a few things he does not like. "When they come in, run towards them. Don't jump up or they'll hit you. Look winsomely into their eyes and they'll stroke you behind the ears. If you do these things and never bark too loudly, they'll feed you and all will be well."

He is unsure, but tries these tricks and they seem to work. He learns more from Dennis. "They like us to be placid and lick their hands. Dogs who are noisy and bite disappear."

He detects lingering scents of long gone dogs. The people say that his name is 'Toby'. He learns to come when they call him. They drop or throw a ball or a stick. When they shout, "Fetch!" they seem pleased, if he retrieves what they throw.

Dennis passes on dark rumors of a terrible place. "They take you to see a man in a white coat. He has rubber hands. His rooms are completely white and smell horrid. Some dogs that go into the room where he works never come out. There's a smell of death.

"He cuts us and makes us bleed. It starts with him sticking in needles. It hurts. He forces us to drink horrible liquids. They wrench your mouth open if you don't want to drink."

Sure enough, one day, the woman puts him in a travelling cage and carries him out into the big red machine. They pull in at a big house with other machines outside. There is a big sign, with red marks he does not understand. 'Veterinary Surgeon'.

* * *

The mistress pushes open a glass door and puts his cage on the floor. He sniffs that lots of other dogs have been here. There are other people with dogs on their laps or in cages. Some other animals and birds are here too. Their odors are pungent and weird. He senses fear and sickness. The hairs on the back of his neck stand up. Wild eyed with terror, he looks through the bars of his cage.

The door of another room opens. He glimpses a white robed man with a knife. A waft of death and illness comes from the room. Toby yelps and shrinks to the back of his tiny prison.

Then it is his turn to go in. The man in the white coat seizes him in strong rubber hands and jabs a needle into him. He barks, to no avail. They force-feed him nasty fluids, just as Dennis foretold.

* * *

Back at the house, he regards fat old Dennis with new respect. He seemed a little stupid before and understands much less of the human language than Toby does. Still he has useful experience. Somehow, he does not have male scents.

Dennis tells him of the day he was castrated. It sounds truly awful. Again there was an injection and then a knife had sliced off his bollocks. Dennis was sore for days after and felt sick. Toby likes to lick those parts. It gives him a mild thrill. He asks, "But why do they do that?"

"I think it's to make us fat and obedient, but I don't really know. Maybe we get fat because they make us share their sweet and sticky foods. We have to beg and look pleased."

Toby listens and learns more human speak. When starving dogs come to the gate, he hears the big people say that it is bad not to castrate them and that they must take Toby to the vet soon. There are too many puppies scavenging and dying on the street. Toby is terrified.

Two sunrises later they load him into the travelling cage. He tries to resist, but they push him in saying, "Bad dog. This is for your own good. Besides it won't hurt."

The mistress drives the big red machine.

* * *

In the vet's waiting room, he sees some different, older women with wrinkled faces and mean pursed lips. They look very determined and intimidating. They bring in frightened and cowed dogs. He notices that these women have very fat and tasty looking rumps and bare legs. From their smell, he knows that humans are made of meat.

The women chat enthusiastically to his mistress "We've collected over fifty street dogs this month so far. The locals don't understand. Castration's the only way to stop the dogs breeding. But there are always hundreds more."

He thinks that these women are ravening fiends. Their eyes glitter when they speak of castration. Toby crouches into the floor of his travelling cage, trying to make himself smaller. He must escape, but how?

Toby's owner is called to the operating room and carries him in. There, she coaxes him out of the cage with a treat. He pretends to come out quietly. The man with the rubber hands strokes his muzzle, holding a syringe in the other hand. Toby leaps forward and bites hard into the rubber. The hand is made of meat too.

The man screams. Toby's mistress slaps him, but he only bites down harder, with a satisfying crunch of bones. The door flies open and the assistant runs in. Toby lets go and bolts for the open door.

The horrible women with the meaty rumps try to catch him. He runs through a narrow gap between elephantine legs. The outer door is shut. He dashes around, yelping. Other dogs bark too. How can he get out?

He is at a loss as to which tempting and massive target he should attack. The woman he chooses cannot see him. He is below the mass of her enormous bosom.

He runs behind her and clamps firmly down into a tasty buttock. She hollers like a stuck pig. One of her friends flees, shrieking as she opens the outer door. Toby dashes after her, pursued by the other women in an angry mob. They cannot waddle very fast and one falls over, tripping his mistress and the nurse. He runs and runs.

He hides in the hedge of a field by the roadside. The machines rumble slowly past. The women lean out of the windows calling his name. He lies low in silence watching from behind some weeds.

* * *

After dark, Toby trots further up the road to the mountain. Whenever a machine's lights approach, he hides by the roadside. Eventually, the street turns into a path into the woods.

Desperately thirsty, he drinks at a stream. In the woods there are many strange odors. He hears animal and insect noises. Some flies bite him. They raise lumps that make him itch. He tries to scratch at them with his hind legs. He finally dozes off on a patch of cool soft moss under a tree.

He smells the dawn before the sun rises. He stretches and walks into a clearing. Big black birds with flapping wings tear at a dead animal. He chases them away, ignoring their protesting squawks. He gorges himself. Sniffing the air, he feels free.

* * *

As the years pass, hunters venturing into the forest tell scary tales of being attacked by a huge hound from hell and a pack of other dogs, some that look like their giant, demonic leader. At first, the bravest hunters go after them, but the devil dogs seem to evaporate into the darkest depths of the undergrowth and the steepest parts of the forest.

People say they must be ghost dogs. Mothers tell wide-eyed children that the dogs will come to get them if they are naughty.

Then, one or two huntsmen disappear never to be seen again. Terrified woodsmen hunt elsewhere.

The End

When the Saints go Marchin' in

"A man is no less a slave because he is allowed to choose a new master once in a term of years."

Lysander Spooner

"Gratitude is a sickness suffered by dogs"

Joseph Stalin

It is 2017, Pete and Carolyn are entertaining their gringo guests on their capacious veranda. It offers spectacular views of the lush, Central American valley below. Their luxurious home is built on the slopes of Volcan No Donde.

Pete tinkles a spoon on his glass to catch everyone's attention. The guests look towards him expectantly, "I'd like you all to drink a toast to our new arrivals John and Janice. We, the other expats on the hill, welcome you both to Calle Mora. We hope you'll have many happy years here."

All raise their glasses and drink. "To John and Janice!"

John, a beefy, red-faced Texan, wearing shorts that fit him fifty pounds back in time and show off his varicose veins to best advantage, replies with a beaming smile. "Well, gee thanks everyone. We feel really welcome. Janice and I'll get round y'all to see how we can fit in and maybe help the community."

The party breaks into small chattering clusters. John confides to a small group of men who nod sympathetically, "We came here because it's cheaper than Houston. Property seemed especially reasonable. We liked the idea of low cost healthcare. They told us the climate was perfect, though the winds last week were a little high. Our satellite dish blew right off the house. Course, we have bigger winds in Texas."

* * *

The following week, Janice, a bleached blonde on the anorexic side of thin with the permanently surprised eyes of one too many facelifts, is sitting next to Cheryl at the 'Cheeky Chicas' monthly women's lunch club. So far, she is pleased to discover that the women are mostly friendly and that they support various charitable causes.

The raucous twang of North American English is overwhelming. There are no Latinas there of course. The group's name is merely to show how well its members like to feel that they have acclimatized to the local culture.

Janice likes to bestow compliments. "Say Cheryl, that necklace you're wearing is really cute. I think that bit of polished concrete around the stone is especially artistic. Did you get it locally?"

"Why no, Janice. Cindy over there platted the cord from twine she bought from the Cabécar.

They're very needy aboriginals and live in the remote Chirripo mountains. Cindy makes the stones herself from recycled floor tiles.

"We all like to help the poor and the natives whenever we can. It doesn't do to wear our real jewellery when they are going hungry. Besides, they might steal it. We keep mine in the safe, with Pete's guns and his gold bars."

"Yes, that's a good idea about the jewellery. I want to join in helping the Latinos too. Any places I should start looking, to help out?"

"Go talk to Linda, the lady to Cindy's left. She has a big heart, and just about everything else too. Come on. I'll introduce you."

They walk round to another table in the café. Linda, a very large woman with a booming voice, is holding forth. She usually is. Her bosom obscures her half eaten chicharrones, the famous Latin pork dish. Janice and Cheryl have to await an opening in Linda's endless diatribe. Eventually, there must come a chance for someone else to speak.

Linda is in full spate. "Well, we sponsored 20 'procedures' on male dogs last month. Latinos prefer males as guard dogs but they take no responsibility for them. Castration really is the only way to stop poor starving puppies dying on the street."

Janice wonders for a moment whether Linda means the Latinos or their dogs, as she continues. "We women prefer to neuter the males than to tackle the fewer females. We females suffer enough in life, don't ya know. Castration also makes the dogs more placid."

Just as Janice feels as though she is about to expire from standing in the humidity so long, Cheryl jumps in to the merest sliver of verbal space with the deftness of long practice. "Linda, this is Janice. She says she'd really like to help you with your project."

A delighted Linda pulls Janice into an empty chair with her enormous arm. Janice looks around surprised, but Cheryl seems to have vanished into thin air. Janice spies her at a far table. 'How did she do that?'

As the luncheon breaks up, they all pose in groups for the obligatory 30 photos for facebook. The same people appear every week somewhere, 'oohing and aahing' over their mutual admiration club.

There are lots of smug marrieds among their Facebook friends, with multiple pictures of anniversaries, birthdays and smiling grandchildren who all look pretty much the same. The couples look mawkishly lovey dovey in every photograph. Single women, like Linda, prefer to publish pictures of their pets wearing silly hats and the like.

Many of the ladies are disaffected with politics in the US or Canada and publish political opinions or copies of articles on social media. They know in their hearts that their home country's political problems are insoluble, so being in distant Central America gets them away from that daily reality. For strange reasons they then revisit the issues from their tropical haven. Some post wistful photographs of the beauties of their home landscapes.

* * *

A month later, Janice and John are quaffing whisky on the rocks, watching yet another spectacular sunset from their terrace. John moves on to beer, scarfing down his fifth slice of pizza. He is trying to speak between cheesy mouthfuls. Janice waits expectantly. He clears his mouth with a slurp from his can of local beer and a belch. "Well this is what it's all about. Look at that sun. How did you get on at the Caja today?"

"Oh Caja, the local universal healthcare? Well the hospital was pretty crummy, but they let us into the system and it's so cheap. Obviously, I kept our pre-existing conditions secret from them.

"The officials are as inefficient as everyone says they are. They only spoke Spanish and took hours over everything. It's a good job Ronaldo the handyman was with me."

"Yeh Janice, it's disappointing. They need us expats to employ them as builders, cleaners, gardeners and the like and yet they make it so hard for us. They tried to charge us for our workers' Caja and labour taxes. At least we got out of that one. We didn't pay our Mexicans' taxes in the US. I'll be damned if I'm paying here."

She nods sympathetically, "They can't even fix the roads. Why should we pay tax? No one else here does."

He grunted, readying himself for another gargantuan bite of pizza. "That's right, and look at all we do for them what with the dogs and teaching English classes, supporting the orphanage and all that. The minimum they could do really is to employ English speakers and run the place more along US lines. At least we provided Spanish speakers for the Hispanics in the services in Houston."

She looks sympathetically at him. "Well the girls tell me you can't teach the Latinos anythin'. They're so slow at the English classes. Cheryl said she tries to teach some of them yoga and meditation. She speaks Spanish you know."

"Say Janice did ya hear that rumblin'? Oh My God! I felt a tremor!"

* * *

Volcanologist Doctor Jorge Rodriguez has been trying to warn the authorities for weeks about pressures and tremors he monitors in Volcan No Donde. He eventually got through to the ministry's permanently-engaged switchboard, but his colleagues in the ministry were unsympathetic. "Look Jorge, you've been wrong before. The Tourism Ministry produced their counter-evidence to yours.

"Too many of our friends' businesses depend on tourists coming to our county. Just between us, I've been told to fire you, if this story gets into the media. Believe me. Everything will be fine."

Dr Rodriguez glances again at the increasing activity in his seismographs. With a sense of utter frustration, he buries his head in his hands.

* * *

Down the hill a ways, in a rapidly darkening hovel with no electricity, a poor Nicaraguan, her husband and their four wide eyed, dirty children are going to bed hungry yet again.

She complains bitterly, "El Gordo in the big car nearly killed us today as we were walking up the hill. He was going so fast that he didn't even notice us. Little Gilberth hurt his arm jumping into the ditch."

"I'll kill the Gringo, if I get the chance."

"Santa Maria! Don't talk like that in front of the kids. God will help us if only we pray enough."

* * *

Next day, Janice is enjoying coffee and carrot cake with Cheryl. They are excitedly talking about the tremor. She spots her gardener hacking chunks off her roses with his machete and screams at him. "Stop that, you idiot!"

She reverts to Spanish, berating him. As she turns to Janice, neither of them notices his sullen glaring at her rudeness. It was in front of another gringa, making the reproach even more unforgivable.

He throws the machete down and fumes to himself in the shade of a palm tree, before resentfully resuming work. He needs the money. But one day she'll pay for treating him like dirt.

He sharpens his machete to a razor's edge, thinking as he makes each stroke against the stone. 'Why do gringos think it's fair and normal to be retired here and me still working at 67 years old and no pension in prospect? I hear that gringos get straight to the front of the queue for treatment in our hospitals, even though they just arrived and never paid into the system before.'

Cheryl waves to some bushes that have been hacked about a bit. "Just look at those, Janice! It's like they've been ravished by a Brahma bull. These idiots aren't gardeners. They only know how to grow coffee. I don't know how many times I have had to yell at him and he still doesn't get it. I'll have to get rid of him, but the last one was just as bad and when he left, half our garden tools went missing."

* * *

At four in the morning, all the dogs for miles around start barking. Seconds later, with a roar like a thousand thunderclaps, the volcano explodes catastrophically. A huge pressure wave shocks all living things across the entire valley.

A mile high jet of molten magma sears into the sky, and then vanishes as clouds of dust, gas and acid obscure everything. The earth trembles and shakes. Glowing rocks and debris tumble down through the murk.

Dr Jorge and thousands of others are wiped from the face of the earth by the pyroclastic flow that sweeps away several villages at 120 mph. It bypasses Janice's hill by a mile, but violently rattles her house for twenty minutes, like the rumbling of a mighty goods train. Pictures and cupboards crash from the walls. Crockery and windowpanes are smashed to smithereens.

Incandescent rocks the size of houses hurtle overhead through the blackness of the dust. They land with massive force bouncing great craters into the landscape and then roll onwards smashing down trees. Houses vanish. Lives are snuffed out. Vehicles explode or are crushed into twisted metal.

Huge landslips block all routes to the area. The airports are inoperable, due to thick clouds of acid volcanic ash. There will be no sun for weeks. Phones and cell phones do not work. All power lines are out. Ruptured water pipes empty. The whole of Central America is affected.

All the Latinos on the hill disappear down to their own homes. Their animals are dying. Crops wither and expire in the choking acid darkness. Everything is a total loss.

Violent earth tremors cause further landslips. Some of the gringo houses on the hill are enveloped. Two gringos leave to see if they can get help from down below. They fail to return.

* * *

Thirty or so frightened expats gather at Pete and Carolyn's house. Several are choking with the acid dust, trying to breathe though dirty rags. Many have red raw eyes. All are filthy. Every one of them is desperately thirsty. Some are ill from drinking contaminated creek water.

They look to the party bore. He is always telling everyone that he is the designated coordinator for the US Embassy, which sends out alerts every time a gringo is murdered, robbed or disappears. No one finds the embassy helpful and the bore's pretence at superior knowledge has become tedious. Now, he is wracked with pain and sobbing. He nurses a badly splinted arm in a grubby sling. He whines, "No one seems to care. Nothing has been heard from the embassy. No vehicles can run, the engines clog with dust. Maybe we should hike down the mountain to the valley. There are people and food stores there."

Pete brandishes his Colt .45 automatic for emphasis. "You're crazy. Any food down there'll have been looted before now. I'm stayin' right here with my own gold and supplies. Besides, we've been so good to the locals, they'll be comin' to help us soon. We must be practically saints to them. Still, if any of 'em look dangerous, I can let em have it with this."

This evinces some serious arguments. The bore moans, "Come on Pete, if you've got supplies we can share em, pool our resources, like the good Bible Christians we always say we are. Like you said 'saints'."

Steeling himself, the fellow steps towards Pete and holds out his good hand for the gun. As others turn expectantly to Pete, he fires once into the air. The next round kicks up dirt near the bore's feet. Pete foolishly takes a further step forward. "Fuck the Bible! Listen to the voice of my .45."

The bore shrinks back appalled by the blasphemy, with his ears ringing from the bangs. He looks down the dark black eye of the barrel. He half expects a lightening bolt to wipe Pete from the face of the earth, but God seemed busy elsewhere today. Pete's finger twitches on the trigger.

* * *

An hour earlier, the Latinos assembled below the hill. As usual, word of the gringo gathering seemed to spread around. Nothing ever bypasses their gossip grapevine.

The man who built the house for Pete hates him. Pete had treated him without respect, barking orders and ignoring his advice. "I know where there will be food and water. Follow me. I kept a key to the back gate."

* * *

Under the cover of the commotion caused by the gunfire and continued grumblings from deep in the earth, he leads the crowd of wiry Latinos onto Pete's property. Many carry sharp-edged machetes. Their usual affable smiles have become thin grim lips and hard eyes. They are dust grey, hungry and desperate. Some of the women are carrying small children. One baby seems to be dead, but the mother still clutches it tight to her bosom.

Pete suddenly spots the mob of shadowy people emerging through the murk like zombies. He notes long machetes hanging ready from their arms. Unhesitatingly, he empties the rest of his magazine into the new arrivals. He then starts to load another magazine.

Several Latinos crumple to the ground bleeding. A shotgun fires from somewhere in the mob. Pete collapses, a look of disbelief on his face. He tries to hold in his torn-open belly, as blood pools around him.

His wife runs to him shrieking. An angry local drags her off him by one arm, holding her up so he can lop off her head with a single swing of his weapon.

The only Latina at the party is twenty years junior to her Gringo husband. She tries desperately to defend him, as he lies bleeding and groaning in the dust. "No, Stop! You know me. I am one of you. He is a good man. He helps you all. He believes in Jesus."

A dusty figure thrusts his long blade into her belly and rips upwards. Another repeatedly slashes down at her man till he stops twitching.

Some gringos try to flee into the murk of the garden. The Latinos enjoy flushing them out and hacking them open, butchering them amongst the ash in the yard. Their screams finally subside. The mountain rumbles again.

* * *

That evening, in the quake-resistant rooms of Pete's house, the locals feast on gringo stew, made with the water cache from his garage, adding some dried beans and rice. Pete's housekeeper showed them where everything was stored and opened the safe. She helped herself to an emerald and diamond ring. It glints dully on her finger in the gloom.

The builder of the house tucks a gold bar into his pants saying to his wife, "We can't eat this, but we can bury it. Maybe it'll be useful later. See! God did provide."

She crosses herself and sucks the flesh from a fat rib. A week before, she had accepted 5,000 colones from El Gordo to feed her family. In return he had demanded a disgusting act, too shameful to remember. She hopes this is his rib, giving it a lick.

A mangy starving dog, neutered when Linda took it to the vet a month earlier, now happily gnaws on one of her huge thighbones, crunching at it to get at the marrow. He seems to remember the smell of this woman and gives a happy yelp.

When the Saints came marchin' in, few of these gringos were amongst their number.

The End

Save the Planet 2

"The living will envy the dead"

Nikita Khrushchev on Nuclear War

Three star general Sherman Blitzer squares his broad shoulders in front of the mirror. He pulls his perfectly ironed tunic straight and smugly regards the rows of battle ribbons on his barrel chest. Steely blue eyes stare back at him from a closely cropped head. It grows out of a bull neck with no discernable boundary from his massive shoulders.

Today is an important day. He has to pitch his idea exactly right to have any chance of success. Today is the day he intends to save the Earth.

Donning and adjusting his cap, he marches briskly from his quarters on his way to a deep conference room, four stories of solid ferroconcrete below the research buildings in Los Alamos. His heels echo rhythmically on the hardwood floor.

He passes two marine guards in the long corridor, smartly returning their salutes. Two other marines swing open the double metal doors so he can enter a grey-walled room with no windows. A female lieutenant salutes and accepts his cap, carefully placing it on a table with others that are already there.

He joins his colleagues from NASA, the Navy, the Air Force, the CIA and the State department who are mingling around the coffee table near the far end of the room. One or two greet him as he moves amongst them.

The Secretary of State calls for order. The heavy blast doors clang shut and are firmly locked from the outside. Her smile embraces them all. "Gentlemen and Ladies, please take your seats."

They each sit behind their nameplate around a horseshoe table. There is no writing material, just jugs of water and glasses. The Secretary of State takes a chair to the side of the open end of the table. A large whiteboard stands in the gap of the horseshoe. An MIT professor with top security clearance holds a red marker pen and looks eager to play his part.

Madam Secretary continues, "Welcome to this, the third of our secret sessions to consider possible military solutions to global warming, pollution and overpopulation. As always, there will be no notes or minutes. This meeting never happened. Once again, my special advisor Professor Wolfie Kriegschanz will moderate our brainstorming.

The Prof wears his signature Harris Tweed suit without a tie. His dark eyes sparkle with intelligence. He opens with a summary of the previous two sessions in a few crisp sentences. He has a slight European accent. Perhaps it is Bulgarian or possibly even Israeli. "Our previous two meetings reached pretty stark conclusions.

In the first, we agreed that there is an unacceptably high probability that without drastic action, global warming, pollution and possibly pandemics would wipe out the continuance of humanity within twenty years.

"Our second gathering determined two things. Firstly, that the US is the only country with the potential resources and dominance to lead any remedial actions. Secondly, the sorry state of our civilian legislature and government is such that there is no hope whatsoever of getting anything useful done in time to avert such a catastrophe."

The Secretary of State nods her approval. The Prof's encouraging smile embraces all present. "In setting the agenda for this third discussion, we agreed to bring ideas for a military solution to the problem. Let us hope that you have all thought of something we can do, to save humanity."

The Prof raises his marker pen and stands by the whiteboard expectantly. As each proponent expounds his or her idea, he records them on the whiteboard and taps equations into his laptop. The supercomputers buried deep in the earth a mile away provide preliminary outcomes from their climate models within minutes.

General Blitzer decides to hold his fire until others have made their suggestions. He is learning which arguments get the most support and rehearses his points, reordering a few.

By the time they break for lunch, various ideas have been floated. Two receive the greatest interest. The Army General proposes 'Operation Mirror Deserts'. It requires a military takeover of the Sahara, the Kalahari and various other empty areas. The US's massive logistics and manufacturing capacity would then be deployed to build mirrored panels over these areas. The resulting atmospheric cooling from reflecting the sun's rays might do the trick.

'Space Mirrors' is the NASA scientist's idea. Launching a number of large rockets seems more practical than building mirrors on the ground. Each rocket could carry modules for a string of mile-wide reflective arrays which would fold out when in space. Then they would do the same thing as 'Mirror Deserts', but use vastly less resources. The other benefit is that all the mirrors could be put into orbit from within US sovereign territory, reducing the risk of global war. One issue is that the mirrors could potentially be used to reflect the sun onto hostile territory. The Air Force likes this capability but others feel that merely building the capability would be casus belli.

Other proposals are advanced to varying degrees of skepticism. Unsmiling, Lieutenant General Blitzer stands up to make his own bold proposal. He waits for silence. "To deal with the problem in time to be effective, we need something that can be implemented before the civilian authorities have the opportunity to interfere and screw it up. I'm talking hours, not the months or even years that would be needed to develop the other ideas we have heard so far. This means we have to use assets we already possess."

The Air Force general arches an eyebrow at him.

He is her kind of man, though she is rather attached to the Mirrors in Space concept. Her eyes strip away his uniform. Maybe she can persuade him to come to her room during the overnight break.

Blitzer continues, "The prospect of getting away with a military solution without support from the Chinese and Russians is highly dangerous and would likely lead to nuclear catastrophe."

This gets a few nods around the table. The Secretary of State interjects. "How can we get them on board without civilian interference?"

The Prof looks pained, "With all due respect Madam Secretary, the rules are that we hear the full proposals before opening discussion."

The others wish they had the clout to call the Secretary of State to order. Few who have publicly challenged her have ever managed to keep their jobs. She reluctantly sits back in her chair, pyramiding her hands and biding her time.

Blitzer ploughs on, "Your point is a valid one Ma'am. We cannot involve civilian governments.

We have to clandestinely involve our military counterparts in China and Russia. They have less of a problem in acting without civilian interference. It is part of the burden of democracy that we bear and they do not. We can deal with our allies ex post."

Noting the nervous glances and suppressed irritation from some others around the room, Blitzer waves calming hands and rushes on. "I know, I know. If anything goes wrong our asses will be in a sling. But if we don't even try, humanity is doomed anyway and that includes us."

There are one or two grim chuckles at his gallows humor. When he arrives at his proposed action, there are shocked gasps around the table.

The next day, after much discussion, he is given the go-ahead to orchestrate a secret approach to the two most powerful sworn enemies of the United States of America, Russia and China.

Following their steamy session the night before, Blitzer requests that the Air Force general, who is fluent in Mandarin and Russian, should be his number two in the project. He looks forward to the secret sessions in both senses of the words.

* * *

As an act of good faith to the Russians, the subsequent meetings take place in the Soviet Embassy in Venezuela. The two American delegates are smuggled from across the Colombian border in Russian diplomatic vehicles with darkened windows.

In a bigger leap of faith, the Americans have to disclose to the Russians that their supposed secure room in this embassy is bugged and that the bugs need to be removed before the meetings. After some anguished moments the Russians take this as the act of friendship that it is.

The Chinese delegation comprises Marshal Chang, number two in the People's Liberation Army and a female colonel as interpreter. They arrive via their own Venezuelan embassy with diplomatic passports giving false identities.

The Russians field Marshal Kunstov head of the SVR RF, the CIA's counterpart. He is accompanied by a Mandarin-speaking major. Much to the chagrin of his Air Force compadre, Blitzer gives the sloe eyed major an appreciative once-over.

Without too much wrangling, they all agree that the Russians are to chair the meeting. As is customary, the Russians propose a vodka toast to the success of their talks as they open proceedings at 8 am.

Overcoming the inevitable suspicions, all the delegates concur relatively easily that a four step military solution is required. There must be an immediate reduction of world population by at least one and preferably two billion, i.e. around a quarter of mankind. A means of drastically reducing the sun's rays from hitting the planet is also essential to the plan.

Over the next few days, the trickiest third and fourth parts of the plan are thrashed out. The military forces of all allies need to be neutralized and immobilized during the main operations. This causes much debate and horse-trading. Lastly, blame for the whole operation has to be directed away from the three 'frenemy' powers at the table.

Over following weeks, the Chinese and Russians readily concede that North Korea will be sacrificed, but Pakistan will only be included if the Americans accept giving up Israel and Saudi Arabia. Piece by piece a new map of the world is being negotiated; one that removes most of the thorns from the various players' sides.

Considerable time is spent on planning the trails of fake satellite and radar information necessary to support the accepted propaganda and posturing that each side will need to deceive its media, civilian governments and populations.

* * *

Two months after the conclusion of negotiations, at 0600 New Delhi time, a preemptive nuclear strike, apparently from Pakistan, takes out all India's major cities and missile bases. Over three quarters of its population is incinerated in the initial blasts. The plan requires that most of the rest will perish from radiation or starvation over the following few weeks. Within ten minutes Islamabad and most of Pakistan's cities disappear too under mushroom clouds, presumably from retaliatory Indian counter strikes.

In Indonesia, the most populous Muslim country, Jakarta, Surabaya, Bandung and Bekasi are obliterated. To all the protagonists' relief, troublesome North Korea ceases to exist.

In the Middle East, Haifa, Jerusalem, Baghdad, Riyadh and Jeddah, followed by Damascus, Tehran, Mashhad and Tabriz are obliterated within the hour or so. Care is taken to reduce all the holy places to sheets of nuclear-fused glass to prevent the possibility of future pilgrimages to these sites. Oil producing areas are spared for later recovery and exploitation.

Greater Tokyo's 70 million population disappears in a flash. Another strike hits Osaka. This is the price exacted by the Chinese in their hard bargaining.

The cover-up goes well. The US provides Britain and France with credible disinformation as to the origins of the nuclear strikes, pointing fingers at Pakistan, Israel and North Korea. The US President, who is in on the plan, insists that the nuclear forces of the UK and France stand down.

In each country, those involved in the strikes are convinced that they are acting under legitimate orders. Amid the ensuing chaos, personnel in the US and Russia who know any details of the plan are already being liquidated by Russian hit squads as their parts in the program are completed.

The dust clouds generated by the 50 or so thermonuclear weapons, mostly American, will block out the sun for months and cool the earth for many years. Amidst the mess, no one is questioning how amazingly free from radiation the strikes are. Only the US has weapons with these characteristics. News channels are blacked out, except for emergency broadcasts.

*** * * ***

General Blitzer and his Air Force paramour are in the situation room in the Pentagon bunker, watching the action as information streams in. Everything so far is going according to plan. They are elated. She gives his meaty thigh a playful squeeze under the table.

* * *

In the next few hours, the Russian death squads begin to deal with people who know too much. None escape.

Blitzer is blindfolded and naked. He lies face up on his bed. His hands and ankles are tied to the bedposts with silken cords. The Air Force general is riding him enthusiastically and encouraging his bucking and writhing with cuts from a horsewhip. Muffled grunts of ecstatic pain escape around the ball gag in his mouth.

The splintering of the door, as it is smashed in, makes her turn. Her face is flushed. Her eyes are wide with excitement. A hail of bullets rips her apart hurling her off Blitzer. As the slugs tear into him, he does not know what is happening.

Only the Secretary of State, who is with the President on Air Force One, survives this cleaning-up exercise.

* * *

Exceeding what was agreed, the Chinese storm the temples in Lhasa and Bodh Gaya, evaporating what is left of the Buddhist leadership, including the troublesome schismatic Dali Lama. His Chinese rival, installed with Party approval, is now unchallenged.

The People's Liberation Army invades Taiwan in overwhelming force. This exceeds the agreement, but the Chinese President sends a one-line message to the US President. "It is time to make life simpler for all of us for the next thousand years."

Russian Spetsnaz commandos raid Kiev. They stage a coup, reinstating a puppet regime. Russian tank armies crash over the borders of Georgia and other territories lost during the previous collapse of the Soviet Empire. No one intervenes. No prisoners are taken. This is a war to end all wars.

* * *

On Air Force One, the President is discussing the incoming status reports with the Secretary of State. "Well your plan was brilliant. Not only have we exceeded our estimated climate and population reduction objectives, but we've also disposed of all the troublesome regimes around the world. Dealing with the Chinese and the Russians will be much simpler now."

Suddenly the plane lurches in a shockwave, wings over and plunges several thousand feet. The President and Secretary of State grip their seats in alarm. Pieces start to fly off the over-stressed airframe.

Deep within the earth's core, the shock of multiple nuclear strikes has disturbed a delicate balance under Yellowstone National Park. The giant caldera, a forty square mile lake of molten lava under pressure, explodes with a force greater than all the nuclear bombs that have just been unleashed. Three hundred cubic miles of molten magma cut through the earth's atmosphere like an enormous thermic lance, ejecting a large part of the atmosphere off into space.

Flaming rocks the size of city blocks rain down across the continental United States, wiping out every major city and killing all life in a radius of over a thousand miles.

The blazing wreckage of Air Force One plummets towards the earth, breaking up. An engine tumbles, with a fire trail of flaming aviation fuel.

Without leadership, the surviving second-strike forces of the US launch attacks on Russia and China. This is in retaliation for what can only be interpreted as their aggression against the US.

The resulting actions wipe out the rest of humanity and cause a general mass extinction. The earth is covered in ice that will last for thousands of years.

The blight that humankind cast upon the earth is over. General Blitzer's plan has certainly stopped global warming.

The End

THE COMING OF THE BEAST

"The bear has the most powerful spirit, because it walks like a man. It is the greatest hunter. It can swim further than the eye can see. It can run faster than any man. It is stronger than a man. It smells us over great distances.

If we succeed in killing a bear, its soul lives for many days in the weapon that kills it. The rituals to set its soul at rest are long and dangerous."

A Yupik shaman

David and his wife Joyce had been married for five years. She was an anthropologist studying the behavior of capuchin monkeys in Central America, specializing in the monkeys' supposed use of tools. He was a freelance investigative journalist whose current project was to expose corruption in the awarding of large construction contracts in Latin America. This was perilous work, but his sunny disposition, non-threatening manner and natural caution had helped keep him safe so far. Joyce worried about him all the same.

It was raining torrents outside their Panamanian home, so they were sitting on the sofa, enjoying pre-dinner rum cocktails as they listened to enormous water droplets drumming on the metal roof. As usual their bodies were close and she snuggled into his chest, tucking her body under his arm. With his free hand he gently stroked her auburn hair. She remembered their early days together.

They had first met in the Phoenician Hotel in Valetta, Malta. This is a grand, white-painted edifice built during the British colonial era. It was nearly midnight and he had been drinking in the bar. Curiously for such a large and prestigious hotel, the bar was rather seedy and male-oriented. A soccer match was showing on the TV.

She had had a frustrating day at her primate study conference. She and several famous academics believed that monkeys only used tools because researchers had taught them how to use stones to crack nuts and sticks to tease out termites. A professor from a prestigious US university had agreed to discuss the matter with her over dinner. It soon became plain that his interest was in her rather than her issue. Angry and frustrated she had left him at the table, deciding that a nightcap was in order.

David had spotted her immediately, as she sauntered in and took a nearby stool. To her obvious embarrassment, someone had clicked over to a quite explicit porno film on the TV. David had noticed her blushing and nervously looking around, ready to leave. He had felt compelled to rescue her, so studiously avoiding any glances towards the screen, he had asked. "Hi, you look like a fellow American, let me buy you a drink."

Grateful for the diversion and feeling an instant attraction to this tall, brown-eyed man, she had let him lead her out of sight of the TV to a booth in a quiet corner. He was witty and well travelled. Both found the other's work interesting. They had hit it off and she had agreed to meet him by the outdoor pool the next afternoon, following the conclusion of her conference. She was to fly back to Panama City the following day.

The blue-tiled pool was modest in area but deep. He was trying to show off by diving in and swimming several lengths under water without surfacing. She had watched his cavorting, somewhat bemused. The water had slicked down the dark hairs against his body. She had never seen such a hirsute man before and generally preferred smooth men, but there was something magnetic about his antics. It was as if he had a hidden power over her.

That evening, after a rather bibulous dinner, she had felt an incredible compulsion to have him in her bed as quickly as possible. It was the best sex she had ever had. He was gentle and focused on her needs.

Next morning, she had awakened cuddled up to his warm back. The shaggy hairs had tickled her mouth and nose. He had stirred, kissed her, then had padded off to make her a coffee.

Six years later, they were living halfway up the lush green slopes of a volcano in Panama. She was still besotted with him. She thought of him as her hairy teddy bear. Indeed, her pet name for him was Teddy.

Feeling the warm glow from her drink, she languidly twined her fingers in his and gestured to the Inuit sculptures on a shelf. They had brought them back from the previous year's field trip to Alaska.

They were carved from a shiny black stone that showed contrasting light grey tool marks. One sculpture was of a fat seal with the face of a native hunter. The other, David's favorite, was of a Yupik shaman shrugging off his outer sealskin clothing and human face to reveal a fierce-look-ing polar bear emerging from within. He said, "You know that trip to Alaska was the best thing we ever did. It was just fabulous."

She smiled, nodding her agreement and kissed him. She ran a finger down the length of his nose. "You have a bear's nose my love."

His eyes twinkled with laughter. "Only in your mind my darling."

* * *

As an anthropologist, she had ensured that the three weeks they spent in Alaska included hiking with a local guide to see the wildlife and scenery, but with two weeks dedicated to living with peo-ple from the Yupik group of Inuit.

Their guide was a renowned tracker and hunter. "My name is Yaqulpak. It means eagle. That is my guiding spirit. It helps me see animals from afar. Most visitors call me Bob."

Initially skeptical but amused by the guide's boast, David became delighted with Bob. He led them right to various elusive species in the vast wilderness. They saw wolverine, foxes, wolves, and on one day, bears. The bears were closer than he had ever imagined possible and maybe closer than intended.

David, Joyce and Bob lay prone, hidden on a rocky bluff watching some grizzlies below through their binoculars. The bears were maybe 100 yards distant and intent on grazing on the sweet, lush sedge grass. They showed little interest in the observers other than an occasional glance upward and a sniff at the strange scents on the air.

David needed to relieve himself. Leaving the others he skirted some bushes. Suddenly, he came face to face with a mother bear and two cubs. They were as surprised as he was.

The mother gave a great roar and charged towards him covering the few yards in seconds and baring vicious teeth. The cubs whimpered, crouching in the bushes behind her.

Hearing the commotion, Bob and Joyce rushed up behind him. Joyce was terrified for David. Bob was unslinging the rifle from his shoulder, but David was between the bear and the gun. David calmly stood still and stared at the bear. He felt strangely relaxed. The huge bear stopped dead, mere feet in front of him. Rearing up on her hind legs, she revealed her six-inch claws. She sniffed at him. Then with a low growl she turned and bounded off at a leisurely pace. Her cubs, with their cute little grey waistcoats, scampered along behind her.

* * *

Their time with the Yupik was another highlight of the trip. The story of David's encounter had caused much gossip among the locals. Bob told him, "You were very lucky, I thought you were going to die. The spirits were caring for you. Our shaman wants to meet you both. This is a great honor. He doesn't normally see outsiders."

Late in the endless arctic twilight, Bob ushered them into a smoky, darkened cabin on the edge of the village. Only a little light filtered in through a screen over the small window. The room was devoid of furnishings other than some sealskin rugs on the wooden floor. A log fire in the grate, hissing and spitting, cast shadows and gave a russet glow to the room. Bob indicated that they should squat down on some of the rugs. They waited in respectful silence for the shaman to appear.

He entered noiselessly from a rear door. His hair was long and grey, his skin old and wrinkled, tanned to a dark walnut. His slitted eyes sparkled with intelligence. He was clad in a pale leather tunic and leggings. Colorful animal designs; suns, moons and stars covered the supple material.

He squatted, silently regarding them intently for a while. He exuded a mesmerizing presence. Then he spoke, slowly in broken English with a soft deep voice. They had to lean slightly forward straining to hear him. His lips creased in a smile that was matched in his eyes. He focused on David "My Yupik name means Bear Spirit. I am pleased to meet another chosen by the bear."

He asked David many questions. Joyce was riveted by the electricity passing between them. Then he reached out, holding David's head firmly between his hands. He remained like this with his eyes closed for maybe a minute, retaining his hold.

Joyce noticed his eyeballs moving rapidly beneath their lids, almost as if in REM sleep. Next he breathed normally and spoke in an eerie voice arising from his stomach. The strange language was interspersed with gruff growls, grunts and snuffles. Sometimes the sound seemed to come from him, but then from different points around the room. It was magical.

Finally, he took a deep breath and opened his eyes, looking intently at David. "You are indeed chosen. You have a spirit gift greater than any I have seen in my 70 years."

He lit a long pipe with a carved walrus ivory stem and shared it with them. David and Joyce were non-smokers and coughed. Bob and the shaman chuckled at this.

That night as they slumbered, they both had the same vivid and colorful dream. They were sleeping beneath the stars. A green Aurora Borealis filled and moved around the entire sky, like a great magic curtain. They were surrounded by three contra-rotating circles of dancing grizzly and polar bears. Next morning, they awoke totally refreshed and content.

* * *

The only blight on their current Panamanian idyll was their neighbor Rodrigo. His sprawling property was slightly screened from their own by a line of pine trees. His family's 15,000 square foot mansion in its heavily fenced compound was perhaps a quarter of a mile further up the volcano.

Rodrigo was infamous and greatly feared by the locals. His daughter drove her black Mercedes 4X4 up and down the road to the houses at a furious pace. Joyce's cleaner confided that she had run over several dogs in the last year and worse had killed a child in the village. Rodrigo was a property and construction multi-millionaire, well connected to both the central government and local law enforcement. Nothing was done.

Rodrigo's sons were notorious drunken bullies and braggarts. The gossips claimed they were connected to the Mexican drug cartels. Nobody dared cross them. Their high-powered motor-cycles and sports cars, with the sound baffles removed from the exhausts, roared up and down the mountain most evenings, often returning in the wee hours from the city nightclubs. The local girls were not safe when they were around.

Their return to the mansion was invariably ac-companied by the barking of frighteningly fierce dogs which roamed their property. The rau-cous intruder alarm often sounded as they blun-dered into their house. Frequent late-night par-ties complete with fireworks and amplified music rendered sleep difficult for all the neighbors. The valley was a natural amphitheater that echoed and increased the cacophony. Sometimes gun-shots and screams were heard.

A peasant farmer had complained to the police after his own dog was torn asunder in the street by three of Rodrigo's enormous mastiffs. The farmer had barely escaped with his own life, his leg lacerated. Two days after the incident he was gunned down in a nearby bar by five men. They escaped on motorbikes. Everyone knew who was behind it and no one dared complain again about the predations of that family.

One evening, David and Joyce were enjoying the sunset from the wicker chairs on their terrace. It was an awesome event. Every warm color in the sun's pallet painted the clouds and sky across the entire horizon. The brooding jungle-clad mountains on the far side of the valley were silhouetted against this wonder of nature.

Joyce looked sadly at him as she caressed the hairs on the back of his hand. "Teddy, I love it here, but I can't stand many more nights without sleep. Rodrigo and his boys are here to stay. Maybe we should just move on."

"I know. It is terrible that they get away with it all. Last time I tried to speak to him about it, he laughed in my face. That was when they sprayed 'Gringos go home' on our gates.

"We also had trouble renewing our residency permits, if you recall. Maybe you're right. But it seems such a shame."

That night David lay in bed, with Joyce molding along the length of his back, as was her wont. The roar of passing high-powered engines was followed by the usual terrible howling and deep throated yapping from above. Rodrigo's burglar alarm screeched across the valley. Groaning, Joyce rolled over and pulled a pillow over her ears. She felt David get up. He often went to use the computer or the bathroom when he was disturbed at night.

The next morning, they were sound asleep when the early morning birds started their sweet dawn chorus. The first light of dawn filtered through the net curtains.

Then, there was a tremendous uproar in the street. Police sirens howled and there was much commotion from the mansion above. Just as they were finishing their breakfast of tropical fruits and coffee, a police vehicle dew up outside their gate. David went to see what they wanted. He was confronted with a tough-looking police captain accompanied by several heavily-armed officers in bulletproof vests. He opened the gate. Joyce came to stand beside him. "How can I help you, officer?"

"You must have heard all the noise and screaming in the night. Why did you not call us, señor?"

"There's a lot of noise every night. What happened? We went back to sleep."

The captain sneered at him in disbelief as his men fanned out across their property, walking towards the perimeter with Rodrigo's land. "Don Rodrigo and his entire family were murdered last night. The dogs were killed and four of his guards too. The rest ran away. You expect me to belief that you, his neighbor know nothing. Don't take me for a fool, señor."

"But it's true this is the first I have heard of it."

Joyce nodded her head supportively, clinging to his arm.

"So you say, señor. We are taking all the neighbors to headquarters for questioning. You will get in the van with the others please. We have ways of getting the truth out of people there."

As the large police van pulled out, David saw white vehicles waiting, with 'Forense de la Policía' painted on the side. Men in white overalls were jumping out and running into his compound.

* * *

David and Joyce were confined separately. He had demanded access to Joyce and to the US embassy. His uniformed interrogator responded laconically, "All in good time, señor. First you will answer our questions."

David sat in a cold, steel chair in front of a metal table in a stark room with paint peeling from its walls. A harsh white light shone directly into his face. Two tough-looking cops, with scars and tattoos, slouched against the metal doorjambs. An immaculately dressed colonel slapped some large, vivid photographs down in front of him one by one. They were truly horrific.

He could see that the bodies had been virtually torn apart. There was blood everywhere. A fat man had had his head ripped off. A woman with her face almost removed had been eviscerated. Some of the shots, showed the remains of the large dogs. David looked puzzled. They bore vicious claw marks and their body parts were strewn around at unnatural angles. The colonel enlightened him. "Their backs were broken."

Then the colonel produced more pictures. These seemed to be showing large animal footprints in the mud and a close-up of part of a fence. There were strands of fur caught on its metal barbs. David recognized another view as being from the fence along his land. The officer gave him a hard stare. "Did you know it is an offence to keep dangerous animals? Where is your beast and what is it? We are going to charge you with murder for this.

"Gringos do not survive in our beautiful prisons. Full cooperation is your only hope."

* * *

A week later, Joyce's situation had somewhat improved and she was back at home. David was still sleeping in a cell at Police Headquarters, but he was presently in a meeting room with a lawyer who had been recommended by the US Embassy and a forensic psychologist. His hands and feet were chained. He looked haggard, from worry and lack of sleep.

The smartly dressed, bilingual lawyer was speaking. "David, things are very serious. The victims were members of a very well-connected family. The president of Panama himself is taking a close interest in the case. The US is not prepared to do much more to help you in the current climate.

"China is investing heavily in Nicaragua to build a rival to the Panama Canal. The Chinese are currying favor with our northern neighbor, Costa

Rica, supplying them with 'gifts', soft loans and infrastructure investments. US diplomats have been instructed to back the current regime here in Panama to counter any Chinese influence.

David looked despondent. "But I didn't do anything. I know nothing about all this. I don't understand any of it."

The lawyer shot back testily. "Look! Everyone knows you were investigating corruption. A lot of people in authority here are very angry about that. They're worried about what you might say in court, if you ever make it that far."

David sat back in his chair despairingly. At least Joyce was not in jail, but she was having to cope with the dangers outside on her own. He raised his hands palms upward in surrender. "What do you suggest I do?"

The lawyer gave him a vulpine smile, "Panamanians are incredibly superstitious. The Police forensic evidence is clearly concocted to play to this. It shows that all the killings were made by a huge brown bear. I cannot believe that myself, but that hardly matters. The prosecutors say that they can prove the bear came from your property.

"The police seem convinced that you kept the bear on the premises as some kind of pet. I have checked and the nearest brown bears to here are in zoos and are all accounted for. Wild ones are confined to the sub arctic circle. Clearly this is all utter nonsense. Somehow they have to be framing you, but this is Panama, not the US. The Panamanians get to decide your fate even though you are an American citizen."

The lawyer shrugged and then continued, "I know, I know. You deny all of this completely, but the Panamanians are determined to convict you. Lack of any cage or bear scat on your land are both in your favor. Remember though, the authorities are not above fabricating as much further evidence as they need. It's the way things work here. Given how ridiculous their case is so far, who knows what they might do next. I'm worried for your safety, because if this gets to a trial, it would make Panama a laughing stock internationally.

Gesturing to his so far silent woman companion he said, "This lady here is a psychologist. Friends in the prosecutors' office tell me that if we deploy her, you can escape with being kept in a criminal mental institution for a while and then released when the fuss has died down. The media here are still full of the story. The public love all this. They are already talking about werebears. It makes a change from werewolves. Please just listen to what she has to say."

The psychologist had been watching them both intently. She now smiled at him and looked at his face with great interest. She knew that there was fame and fortune in this for her. A fat publisher's advance was already in her Cayman Islands account and she had the promise of a movie script to follow. Her book would confirm all the age-old fears embedded in the dark recesses of the human psyche, a guaranteed best seller.

She began eagerly. "The police have your wife's testimony. It is really helpful. She told them that you visited brown bears in Alaska last year and that you took some hallucinogenic drugs with the aboriginals.

"We will argue that this caused a rare psychosis, which we call clinical lycanthropy. Lycanthropy is a word for a man turning into a wolf, but we psychologists apply it to any animal. I can cite twenty previous cases recorded in our professional journals, but none is as interesting as this. Our defense will be that you believed that you had actually become a bear and committed the murders, whilst you were out of your mind."

The lawyer interjected, "You might have to throw a fit of rage in court to substantiate the story, roaring and all that. We will prep you. Meantime, bears are being reported all over the place. This will all give credence to our argument."

David snapped back, "But that's all totally ridiculous. What about the forensic evidence of actual fur and grizzly bear DNA?"

The lawyer interjected, "Don't worry, the prosecution will make all that disappear. Why they concocted it in the first place beats me. The authorities assure us that if you plead insanity they will limit your confinement. This is your only hope. Think of your wife. What do you say?"

* * *

The world's media had descended on Panama in force. The story was catching the headlines around the globe. Even the serious papers were giving it the front page.

All through the night, vehicles and satellite dishes were being deployed around the outside of the 'hospital' for the criminally insane, where David was incarcerated before being brought to trial.

As dawn broke, two burly psychiatric nurses in white coats plodded along each corridor inside the facility on their morning rounds. They looked through the small trap in each heavy steel door to check that their insane charges were still living. Some inmates were confined in chains or strait jackets.

As they reached the last corridor they rushed forwards. The door of cell 11 that contained the crazy gringo had been wrenched off its hinges and tossed to one side. He was gone. One nurse blew his whistle. Others came running. Alarms sounded.

A major investigation was started to find out who had helped with the breakout. The sleeping security guard in the control room was arrested. The CCTV cameras in the relevant corridors had all been ripped from the ceilings.

Joyce was a prime suspect. A large police convoy careered up the steep mountain towards David and Joyce's compound raising a cloud of dust, engines roaring in low gear. As they neared the gate, they saw the rear ends of two large bears bounding off into the rain forest.

They used a tractor to tear off the metal gate with a steel hawser. They rushed around the house weapons drawn, but there was no sign of either David or Joyce.

Other cops unleashed their dogs at the edge of the jungle, but they would not enter and remained barking at the edge. Afraid.

The End

Twilight of the Gods

"Look around at all the war and suffering. Look at the sinful and hurtful nature of humanity. Some people are total monsters but no one is without sin. Clearly only Satan could have created this flawed and evil world we live in."

Translated from the secret 10th century *Testament of Bogomil*, monk and heretic.

There is infinite total blackness and nothing material within it. So it was before. So it is now. So it always will be. Two disembodied bundles of thoughts, call them 'minds' if you will, fill the same space, fill no space, fill all space.

A tiny speck called earth briefly existed in a corner of a multiverse, which itself had flickered fleetingly in infinity. Perhaps because the minds are disembodied, the multiverse only existed within them and was never embodied either.

The beings of earth gave names to these minds. The beings were ignorant, but maybe some of them were able to instinctively sense the minds. If so, that was because one or both of the minds willed it so.

The earthlings saw conflict between the minds. In different eons of earth time, muddle-headed beings called the mind that created the universe, Moloch, Shiva, Belial, Satan and a thousand other names. The opposing mind force was given many names too: Vishnu, Yahweh, Jehovah, Allah and others.

Mostly, earthlings were confused, but were always striving to seek the unknowable. They were so because one or both of the two of the minds willed them thus.

We can refer to the minds as Evil and Good, though that is a gross oversimplification. Both minds just are.

*****

In the blackness and occupying the same space and no space, the two minds grappled. They disputed over their game that had included the multiverse and encompassed the brief existence of the infinitesimal earthlings.

"I won the game. I made the multiverse. You tried to change it and it didn't work. It was consumed by the evil power that I embedded in it. I won the game."

"Nonsense, I won the game. Many wonderful things existed and enjoyed life, even if briefly. That happened because I made it happen. I won the game."

"All right I'll demonstrate."

Evil conjured an apparition. Perhaps it was a replay. It may or may not have had substance. "See. Here is the planet Zort from universe 107,096,509. Your attempts to change it were futile. All your efforts to manipulate the game to allow the evolution of benevolent life forms failed. My destructive beings wiped them all out and then themselves along with the whole planet".

"You are illogical and wrong. One or a billion examples can prove nothing."

"All right, you choose the example and let us see what it proves."

"Fine, then I chose earth"

* * *

Good's mind conjures a frolicking pod of dolphins surfing the waves. For millions of years, that passed in an instant, they sport joyfully in the bountiful ocean. On one day, the sun shines on a calm surface. Mothers tenderly suckle their young. Many in the pod hurl themselves skyward pirouetting and twisting with delight. The warm rays reflect from their sleek skin.

Good reveals the beautiful things they sense with their sonar, hearing, touch, smell and taste. The way they communicate in the most advanced language in the universe is itself wondrous.

Evil conjures a mighty tempest. The swirling black clouds are rent by flashes of lightening. The seas boil and churn. A baby dolphin and its mother are blasted and torn asunder by a million volts.

Good shows the dolphins the calm beneath the surface and a ball of tasty sardines. They dive away from the storm.

Evil shows the terror of the sardines. They desperately flee for their lives, only to be impaled and ripped apart by sharp teeth.

Good moves the scene to the sea in a place called Japan. Two dolphins are supporting a man who was pitched off a typhoon-tossed boat. The dolphins' empathy causes them to gently bear the man to safety on a sandy beach.

Evil moves time forward to the same beach a year ahead. Men are herding the dolphins into nets and stabbing at them with spears. The sea is red.

The dolphins scream in agony. Their entrails are torn from their living writhing bodies. The beach is lined with eviscerated corpses. The men laugh and joke as they butcher the friends of man.

Good objects angrily. "You twisted evolution to create man, the worst monster of all. That was the most horrible thing you ever did."

"I know, that's because I'm smarter then you. Ha!"

"But I still beat you. I gave man curiosity, science and the ability to shape the environment."

Evil demonstrates his opposing view in a time that took no time at all. The Chin emperor, Caesar, Genghis Khan, Napoleon, Hitler, Stalin and Mao flash through the eons. The earth soaks up the gore from piles of heads. Ditches are filled with starved and mutilated corpses.

The wonders of science enable swords, explosives, poison gases, carcinogenic chemicals, man-made diseases and nuclear explosions. Billions suffer from man's greed, aggression, fear and ignorance.

The twisted, bloody, screaming bodies of count-less holocausts zip though the two minds. "You won? I don't think so."

"Well some humans saw the truth. Look."

Bogomil, a hooded monk in Bulgaria, preaches to a crowd. "The devil created everything. Only by praying to the good god can we be saved and help him fight the evil one."

"Saved? Pah! What a ridiculous idea. What ar-rogance, that they thought they had any impor-tance at all. See what happened."

Two centuries of crusades cooked up by crooked popes and Hungarian kings, crazy for power and gold, whizz by. Thatched villages burn. Infants are tossed into the flames, their mothers raped by brutal soldiers. Men are broken on the wheel, their joints smashed to bloody pulp by black-hooded executioners with huge hammers.

"Hang on, look. Sense this." The new images are feelings: the warmth between a mother lemur and her infant, the caring of a human nurse for an old lady, a chimp rescuing a butterfly from the surface of a pond in gently cupped hands and releasing it to flutter away."

"That's enough! Let me remind you how I ended this multiverse that I created." A large hadron collider appears under a Chinese desert. It is a 70 kilometres long circular tube of magnetically controlled plasma. The power from three massive cities is diverted to drive it. Sub-atomic particles collide and fragment, some travelling backwards in time.

"You interfered with the smaller collider called Cern in Switzerland, but I had the Chinese build this bigger and better one.

"You gave them insights into quantum mechanics to help them understand their pathetic existence. I encouraged them to switch it on. They knew full well that there were dangers of creating small black holes during those experiments. You had some of them warn the rest that there was a chance of small black holes growing beyond control.

"I gave them arrogance, the recklessness and the egos to ignore that possibility. They went ahead and pushed the start button anyway. The universe and all the multiverses vanished screaming into that black hole. I won the game and that's it!"

"Cheat"

"Loser"

"You Horror"

"Fool"

"Trickster"

"Idiot"

"Simpleton"

"OK, look. Let's try it all again. How about the best of three?"

"Fine by me. You'll lose again though."

"Well it's my turn to start."

The End

POSTSCRIPT

My Royal Marine friends, various Buddhist teachers, business coaches and mentors have often told me that I think too much for my own good. This volume is the result of a mixture of an over-active imagination and those irritating thoughts that stop you getting on with life and from ignoring all its inconsistencies and horrors.

These attempted forays into black humor get many plots out of the way without the effort of having to write full-length novels. They also deal with the awkward problem of having eliminated key characters in a single chapter.

There is a tradition in British humor that may be absent in the United States. Brits see amusement in the darkest situations. The Monty Python sketch of death calling at the dinner party where everyone is expiring from food poisoning is a good example. Evelyn Waugh's brilliantly acid observations of snobbery and the ridiculous in his wonderful novels, 'Brideshead Revisited', 'Scoop' and 'Black Mischief' are other examples.

Below are a few comments on each of the stories for those who like to know why narratives are written. Hopefully, the doubts these gloomy tales are meant to cast in the minds of the self-obsessed and smug are plain from the tales themselves.

Save the Planet 1

Our reward for leading an ordinary life of relative success is to be condemned to live with others in the same boat. There are tremendous guilt feelings associated with being born in a lucky place, with loving parents, free education, plenty to eat, full employment and freedom from all but the aged ones' memories of wars and hardship. Education and the media reveal that most of the world's population enjoys no such luck.

Sadly, few of us have the strength of character or the charity to take our wealth and distribute it to the poor. As we grew older our revolutionary tendencies became subsumed by desires for ease, comfort and tranquility.

We are hypocrites. That is why this story is a tongue–in-cheek view of complacent contemporary attitudes.

The idea that we hold the future of the planet in our own hands seems arrogant. This is why I decided to negate Lenny's attempts to save the planet with an asteroid strike. These strikes happen every now and then and can cause mass extinctions.

Homage to Coming up for Air

Whilst still at school, I read all of George Orwell's novels. The fact that to this day they are etched into my memory is an indicator of the power of his writing. In "Coming Up for Air", Orwell portrayed a man who attempted to return to his idealized memories of the England before

World War I. In homage to Orwell, this story is what I imagined a man might have felt on returning to my own childhood home.

Last time I visited Rochdale, I was struck by how clean it was. The absence of the smoking chimneys of the mills was part of this. Many were demolished by Fred Dibnah, the eccentric steeplejack. He became a TV personality by driving round the North of England on a steam traction engine and blowing up brick mill chimneys (check him out on YouTube).

The Clean Air Act of 1956 phased out coal fires in private houses. Steam trains were replaced by diesels in the early sixties. The smoke and smog is gone. Many old sooty buildings were demolished. Others were cleaned. The need for spittoons ended.

I was surprised by the influx of South Asians and their mosques to Rochdale. An important point here is that, as a child, the first person of color I saw was a black nurse who cared for me in hospital. I adored her. There was only one lad of

African and one of Asian origin in my school of 650 boys.

Impressions can be dangerously deceptive and exaggerated. In a recent census, the Asian population of Rochdale was only about 12% and those claiming to be Islamic only 15%. These percentages are more than double those for the UK as a whole, but hardly reflect my impressions.

There are many ethnic East Europeans living in Rochdale too. Some of my best friends at school were the sons of Poles who came to Britain to fight in World War II or to avoid communism afterwards. Others have arrived more recently.

The mugging and hospital scenes, complete with the Irish drunk, reflected my own mugging 20 years ago, when I foolishly tried to fight off three thugs in London.

Red Rory's Nightmares

Having an Irish granny myself, I have always empathized with those who fought and died for the freedom from Saxon and Norman oppression.

It is interesting to meet the many Americans, several generations post-immigration and some with tenuous Irish ancestry, who feel the same way. We all need a sense of our history.

Whilst we were living in New York, a neighbor of Irish descent lamented the days when there was a whole row of Murphies in his class at school. In creating the register scene, I also recalled my own school in Northern England and the taking of attendance in Mary O'Malley's hilarious play, 'Once a Catholic'.

As to the nature of Red Rory's dreams, they partly mirror my own rebellious youth as a socialist revolutionary, before I sold out to the capitalists. My novel *'Revolution'* reflects what I wish could have happened, had things been different. It includes a model of how socialism and capitalism could co-exist without the inequality we have today. I still believe that this could work.

With my good friend and fellow author Mike Crump, I decided to write a tag-team book review of Hilary Mantel's novel, *'A place of greater safety'* about the French revolution of 1789. This review can be seen under book reviews at Penmanhouse.com.

Reading Mantel's meticulously researched book reminded me of the horrors of the Great Terror. In addition it brought to mind that all revolutions have resulted in counter-revolution, civil war and repression. My research files are filled with many examples. Rory's first nightmare is closely modeled on the Great Terror set in Paris over two hundred years ago.

I Lust Therefore I Am

The French have always impressed me with their sangfroid about sex, which we Anglo Saxons make such a fuss about. Jacques is a mélange of several randy Frenchmen I have known and perhaps secretly envied.

Recently, Ivy and I took a long vacation in Europe, including a time with friends in Southern France. During our months in the UK, I was crippled by a mysterious and extremely painful form of arthritis. It resulted in a plane journey exactly similar to that Jacques experienced with Iberia, menu, booze and all. Ivy decided that all my pains were due to the wages of sin, inspiring Giselle's dialogue in the story.

Fortunately, my medications and physiotherapist have since done much to restore my health. In writing this tale, I thought, why waste a horrible episode in my life.

Gone But Not Forgotten

We have been fortunate to dwell in four continents and have travelled the world extensively. The pleasures and tribulations of expat life are well known to us.

We retired to Central America four years ago. As always in expat communities, people leave, usually for very sound reasons. Good friends of ours decided to abandon our adopted country. The shunning that they experienced and the unsettling effect their departure had on us inspired me to write a piece for a local on-line news sheet and this story.

Passing It On

This is a true story. I was suffering from arthritis in a UK supermarket. A lady, who had lost her husband a week previously, sat next to me exactly as in this tale. As always when somebody shares their grief, she felt a little better and I felt the hell of a lot worse.

The Call of What's Left of the Wild

Viscerally, I feel that all animals should be free and wild. As a boy I loved Jack London's doggy books, 'The Call of the Wild' and 'White Fang'.

There are a number of militantly evangelical women who live in our expat community. These good ladies no doubt feel genuine empathy with the starveling and maltreated dogs that roam our streets. I was happy to donate to their animal charities, until it became clear that they were collecting money in order to castrate dogs.

This way of dealing with the problem may have logical merit. However, some of the women have been abandoned or maltreated by men and this story is the result of my suspicions as to those women's motives as well as a male's understanding of what the poor animals go through.

Dogs are slaves to man, who knows what they really think?

When the Saints Go Marchin' In

In the area where we have retired, gringos live a life of parties, barbecues and ease. The locals are mainly poor and eek out a living from coffee farming or serving we rich, lazy foreigners.

Many neighbors bleat about how good they are to their help and how much work their retirement funds provide for the local poor. They are likely honest in these beliefs.

We live on part of the Pacific Ring of Fire, where volcanic eruptions are frequent. A tour guide told me how, when he was ten, he experienced a dramatic eruption, though less catastrophic than that described in the story, he described the experience as traumatic. There was nothing to eat, their cattle slowly starved to death and the family became itinerant share croppers.

It amused me to strip away the fallacious conceit of our expat beliefs, in particular of being good for the locals. Also, I had just read a short story by British comedian Alexei Sayle, "The Mau Mau Hat". In this story, the Mau Mau independence fighters in Kenya target the white settlers. The servants of the kindest settlers are the ones who marked their masters' families out for slaughter.

Save the Planet 2

After writing 'Save the Planet 1' for this book, it was clear that nothing will ever be accomplished by we fat slugs of relatively well-off people and our broken democracies. The military solution seems a plausible alternative.

We live at a time when the lunacies of the military industrial complex, as enacted by the CIA and the generals in Washington, know no limits. This inspired my plot.

The Yellowstone Park caldera has been written up as a massive threat by volcanologists. The ending of the human era through nuclear war and volcanic eruption is one of many possibilities that may trump humanity's own attempts at self-destruction.

The Coming of the Beast

The description of a neighborhood in a corrupt, developing Latin American country is pretty accurate. We know of people driven crazy by the lawless behavior of the rich elites and their ungoverned dogs.

This year, we saw a wonderful BBC documentary 'Inside the medieval mind'. It described what life was like before science largely dispelled our myths of werewolves, dog-headed people and other superstitions.

But these superstitions still exist in the form of bigfoot, yetis, goat-suckers and things that go bump in the night. Werewolves and, as I was delighted to discover, werebears are common in modern fiction, hence this fanciful tale.

Twilight of the Gods

We live amongst various folk who want to convert the local Catholics to their particular form of Christianity. Previously, we travelled in Islamic countries and met very kind Moslems, whilst witnessing the extreme behavior of others. In Asia the panoply of beliefs and religions is as great as elsewhere.

Having studied Catharism and its Balkan and Persian antecedents, the idea of a devil creator at war with a good god seemed as plausible as any other creation myth, i.e. not very.

To demonstrate human insignificance, the idea of two gods, with the personalities of five year olds seemed droll. The destruction of earth by a black hole created in a particle accelerator is seen as a real risk by some eminent physicists.

* * *

To end these explanations let me share the perspective of my Buddhist friends. They say that life is about pain, suffering and death. They claim that they have the solution to dealing with this. Maybe they do.

An alternative view is that, if this is the case, why not kick back and enjoy the parts that are fun. As death is inevitable, why worry about it, or fear it? It would be exceedingly boring to die of 'natural causes' and miss out on any upcoming mass extinction.

If only I could be a toastmaster, dressed in a tropical tuxedo. "Ladies and gentlemen, please charge your glasses. We will toast the apocalypse at zero. Please join me in the countdown."

All "Five, four, three, two, one, Cheers!"

Thank you

On behalf of the author and Penman House Publishing, thank you. We appreciate your support.

Reviews are the life's blood of publishers, authors and help inform other readers. They act as signposts on the literary landscape.

Please take a moment and leave a review of this book on Amazon, GoodReads or wherever readers gather.

Other Books from Penman House Publishing

By Aaron Aalborg -

<u>They Deserved It</u> –- A novel of lust and Revenge Spanning the Centuries Currently available

What is the mysterious Egyptian casket that links murderers over a thousand years?

This thriller begins as a historical novel set in 17th Century Italy, a time of superstition, plagues and cynical exploitation of young women.

It is a ripping yarn of illicit love, hundreds of poisonings, the inquisition, torture and witch burnings, built around true events.

Characters include: Beautiful girls oppressed by dynastic marriages to aged husbands, an attractive and tormented young priest, Machiavellian cardinals and a scheming, atheist pope.

In the second part of the story, the descendants of some of the original characters are driven to fulfil their ancestral destiny in modern day New York. The results include grisly killings, global pursuit, international espionage and a thrilling climax of mass murder, authorized by the President of the United States.

It is up to you to decide which of the victims deserved their fate.

<u>Revolution</u> – Available Now- A thriller to change the world.

This is a must read novel for anyone who really wants to change the way the world is run. It describes a violent revolution in the near future. It begins in the United Kingdom and blossoms into worldwide mayhem.

Three radical students were radicalized in the late 1960s, but after violent experiences bide their time till they are in positions of power. In They assassinate members of the British Royal family and world leaders, before seizing control in a series of credible and stunning acts of violence.

Counter revolutionaries attempt to strike back. This is a frighteningly realistic view of what could happen in today's uncertain and dangerous times. It is of compelling interest to those of the political left and right, military specialists, radical economists and all those who enjoy a twisting turning plot with many surprises.

<u>Terminated Volume 1</u>- From the Slums to the <u>Falklands War</u>-Currently Available

Revelations from recently declassified government archives drive the start of this thriller in two parts. Alex, a talented lad from the most deprived part of Scotland, overcomes the disadvantages of his birth to play a key role in Britain's victory over Argentina in the Falklands war.

He also becomes a successful businessman. The corruption and evils of corporate life are exposed through a series of exciting events.

Terminated is for those who like cliff hanging thrillers and anyone interested in the world of big business, management consulting and war.

Terminated Volume 2- Expected Early in 2016

Thwarted by sociopathic colleagues and corrupt partners, Alex turns his expertise in killing to hunting down and murdering those who fire him, over a number of years and in a variety of painful and unexpected ways.

The exposure of the dark realities of the corporate world continues. The reader has to judge Alex's actions, character flaws and whether the surprising ending is justified.

This is bedtime reading for serial killers.

By Michael Crump –

<u>Candyman's War</u>

A thriller going well beyond the genre, "Candyman's War" is narrated from within the history of the most violent civil war of the Americas.

The story depicts Candyman's transformation from a grad student to guerrilla and, following his "war," to something else entirely. He is already an enigma when we meet him at the border with Mexico.

A Q'echi Mayan, an evangelical Christian and a scientist, he returns home to find a site for botanical research. Radicalized by what he finds in the indigenous villages he leaves then returns to Guatemala. The decision puts him into the center of the struggle with unplanned consequences for himself and the ruling junta. The story is told years after by his closest friends in Monteverde, Costa Rica.

The Oligarch

The second novel of the three-part series, Los Chapin!

Wilhelm Hoffman's mission is to pick up the fight that murdered his German father and his brothers. Returning from a residency in the United States, he takes his assigned post in a small hospital near the western highlands of Guatemala. Within a week he is introduced to the escalated violence of the 14-year civil war. His stepmother, an Indio Indio woman who raised him from his first day knows he is not cut out for the fight. But William, as he calls himself now, persists and reveals a rift in his oligarch family as wide as the country's own social chasm.

A "Surrogate War" for the U.S., the gut issues in the Guatemala Civil War reveal the oligarch's willingness to do anything to maintain their inherited entitlements. William's highly placed uncles suspect his commitment to the oligarch government and plot to reveal him from his first day back.

Treachery, courage, persistence and the power of love pervade this rich tapestry of family history that follows the historical events themselves.

William's highly placed uncles suspect his commitment to the oligarch government and plot to reveal him from his first day back. Treachery, courage, persistence and the power of love pervade this rich tapestry of family history that follows the historical events themselves.

K. Francis Ryan

The Echoes Quartet

An adult paranormal mystery series set in the present.

Echoes Through the Mist – Available Now

Julian Blessing's high-octane Wall Street career is likely to land him in prison. The economy is rapidly melting down. His ex-wife wants him dead and some Russian mobsters share her sentiments. And that's just today.

Julian thinks now would be the right time to start listening to the voice only he hears. The words Julian hears bring a message as emphatic as it is baffling and propels him to a village on the rugged coast of Ireland.

A madman possessing supernatural powers wants to sow terror in the hearts of those in the village. His craving for revenge and his limitless greed put Julian directly in his path. By protecting the village, Julian puts himself high on the madman's to-be-slaughtered list.

Desperate for any advantage, Julian discovers the Hagan, a woman with vast supernatural gifts who is steeped in Ireland's ancient wisdom. Hers are otherworldly talents with decidedly this-worldly applications.

Victims are multiplying fast as Julian races to unlock the Hagan's mysterious arts. Her arcane knowledge is the only hope he has of drawing his fellow villagers back from annihilation. To stay alive long enough to use what he learns, Julian must trust his heart to a stranger, his soul to a witch and place his life in the hands of a village full of Irish lunatics.

Echoes Through the Vatican – Available Now

A shadow organization, tracing its dark ancestry back two thousand years, wants only one thing from Julian – Assassinate the Pope, the leader of 1.2 billion Roman Catholics.

A corrupt cardinal, an honorable priest, a sadistic mobster, a whorehouse madam and a stymied police inspector – They all want something and that something is Julian Blessing.

The loss of everything Julian would give up his life to protect is the outcome if he fails to navigate the deadly maze of Vatican intrigue.

With everything at stake, what if you lose? And what of the Jesuit Book?

Echoes Through Ireland – Coming Soon

Battered physically, spiritually and emotionally, Julian returns to Ireland where his future holds a mixture of recovery and revenge.

Echoes – Coming Soon

All titles are sold exclusively through
Amazon.com

ABOUT THE AUTHOR

Aaron Aalborg is the penname of a writer with many and varied experiences, who chooses to remain anonymous. Born in the North of England, he has variously been a trainee Monk, a student activist, a Royal Marine Commando, a visiting Professor at a European Business School and a successful businessman and global CEO. He and his wife have lived in Asia, Europe and the US and travelled to all the major and some smaller countries, doing business in most of them. He currently resides in Central America.

Made in the USA
Las Vegas, NV
08 March 2021